FROM THE PAGES
OF A

FROM THE PAGES OF A Diary

RAJ DHAR

PARTRIDGE

A Penguin Company

ISBN: Softcover   978-1-4828-1217-6
               Ebook   978-1-4828-1216-9

Partridge books may be ordered through booksellers or by contacting:

Partridge India
Penguin Books India Pvt.Ltd
11, Community Centre, Panchsheel Park, New Delhi 110017
India
www.partridgepublishing.com
Phone: 000.800.10062.62

CHAPTER 1

"Mama my ear hurts"

Nikki's mournful cry woke me from my usual reverie, Nikki my four year old darling had developed ear problem—The doctor had diagnosed a leaky left ear due to some infection at birth. I knew I will have to immediately attend to her ailment or else her pain would become unbearable. I unfastened the seat belt and stood up to reach for the rack just above my seat to get her ear drops from my bag. The economy class seats in a plane are rather too cramped up and free movement is greatly hampered. With great difficulty I managed to fish out a little pouch from my bag and took out the medicine. Quite like me, Nikki has great patience and fortitude to endure pain but today she must be in great pain to complain. I look her in my lap and put some drops of the medicine in her ear and gently rocked her. My head buried in her soft hair, I held her tightly close to my breast.

She was my world, the essence of my being. Before her birth I had not imagined that a tiny frame born out of my body would become the center of my life. I can never thank God enough for gifting me my precious baby. The travails, the tribulation and the humiliation I had to endure from all quarters before her birth seemed to dissolve and vanish when I held this little bundle wrapped in a white cloth close to my bosom "my baby, my child, you are worth the pain I have gone through". Nikki's birth had been a miracle, for her father had given up the hope of ever siring a child. It is amazing the trick god plays on human beings sometimes. He did become a father but it was not through his wife but me; a woman he had loved clandestinely, and lost.

My life took a dramatic turn after Nikki's birth. As soon as I left the nursing home I brought Nikki home; my first priority was to ward off the media that was hounding my house and office to confirm the news of baby's birth. I had decided that I will not allow my baby to be exposed to the paparazzi. Why my child should be punished for my celebrity status! If had to find safe haven for my child and myself, I will have to leave Mumbai. I knew that my life would never be the same again, but I was ready to face any eventuality

I vividly remember that night when I quietly carried my baby into my arms and stepped into the waiting SUV outside my apartment. Reena, my dearest friend and confidante was waiting for me in the vehicle; we drove straight towards the Santa Cruz Airport. She had used her connections to have the SUV driven straight towards the four seater plane owned by her friend; the famous industrialist, Sushant Bhoumik.

After three hours flight, with a brief halt at Palm Airport, we landed at Pathankot airport in Punjab. From the airport, we hired a taxi to take us to Dalhousie in Himachal Pradesh where Reena had arranged a beautiful villa. The five hours hilly journey from Pathankot to Dalhousie was rather tiring and Reena was very quiet and so I drifted into a fitful sleep, with the occasional stirring of the baby waking me up. Occasionally I would look at Reena wondering, what is she thinking! Is she regretting her decision to help me escape from Mumbai!

If Ashwin ever found out Reena's part in taking me out of Mumbai or helping me to relocate to Dalhousie, he will never forgive her. God alone knows how it will affect their relationship. Will he break his ties with her; No No; I don't want to think about it! I pushed the thought of Ashwin out of mind. I have to look ahead of me.

If I say the house in Dalhausie was good, it would be understatement. It was the most beautiful cottage I had ever seen; situated in the upper Bakrota Area of Mall and surrounded by tall pine trees and rippling water coming down from an underground stream and flowing out through a crevice into the ground. This was an idyllic surrounding and had the peacefulness that I needed at this point of my life. The cottage belonged to Dr. Sarojini Thakur, an old friend of Reena. Sarojini was living in U.K. and occasionally visited India. During my visit to the U.K. last year for a book release, I had been instructed by Reena to visit, Sarojini. She was a famous surgeon. She had chosen to settle in London with her children after the death of her husband. This house was an anniversary gift from her husband, Dr. Vikram Thakur and both husband and wife used to spend a few months of the summer in Dalhousie while he was alive. What I liked the most about the house was its isolation, there were no houses nearby and the second house from here was almost two hundred meters away. This would give me perfect obscurity that I needed to hide from the public gaze; I thought and felt happy with my surroundings. It did not strike me at that point that I could not hide forever from the world sooner or later people would find me.

Reena had arranged an elderly couple to help me run the house. This Nepalese couple named Tikka Lama and Neema were the care takers of Sarojini's cottage and lived in the outhouse. They were warm people and I instantly liked them. If they had recognized me from the many pictures flashed on the T.V or in magazines, they gave me no inkling; perhaps Reena had given them some story about me. After unpacking and washing Reena and I went into the sitting room; another beautiful sunny room with its French windows, through which the sun rays gleamed into the room throughout the day, presenting a riot of colors on the carpeted floor. We sat down on the cane chairs before the windows, sipping the tea.

At last Reena said, "Well, Sukriti, so far so good, we have accomplished the most difficult part, taking you and the baby out of Mumbai without anybody getting to know of it but it was not easy for me. Mummy kept asking me yesterday where I was going; why I would not attend Ashwini's birthday party. All I could tell her was that one of my patients in Delhi needed me to accompany her to London for a few days. Mummy believed me but Ashwini looked suspiciously at me but said nothing".

"Ahem' I cleared my throat, this conversation about her family always made me uncomfortable. I felt so wretched and miserable at having involved my dearest friend in my deceit. If she had not she supported me in this crisis of my life; I don't know what could I have done without her!

She went on unmindful of my silence "Ashwin would not rest easy. He will discreetly try to get to the truth. I only hope he does not suspect that I am with you".

I did not want to hear the name of Ashwin being uttered before me. I had totally detached myself from this name. It was like putting a big slab of ice on that part of my past, which was associated with him. Reena had noticed my lack of interest in this conversation, she changed the topic and we began to discuss the weather conditions, the house and the financial issue which I will have to sooner or later confront, if I had to stay here without any work or any regular source of income.

Later that night as Reena and I sat together pouring over the various files I had brought with me concerning my bank accounts, money transfers, her cell phone rang, we looked at each other, startled, who on earth could call her at this time, had she not acquired a new number which only her mother knew. Who could it be! Reena answered it.

I could hear the angry voice of Ashwin. "Reena, where are you? I had to force mama to give me your number, what is happening. I know you are not in Delhi."

"Dada I am not in Delhi" Reena said, "But why did you call, I hope all is well!" she asked. Suddenly the baby gave out a loud wail; she was lying in the cot and it was her feeding time.

"Reena I can hear wailing of an infant, who is it.' Ashwin inquired.'

"Dada it is the TV program". Reena said to appease Ashwin.

I picked the baby and went out of the room not wishing to overhear the family conversation. After all I had no interest in any of her family members.

Reena left by a taxi the next morning for Pathankot from where she had to catch the flight to Delhi. After her departure I felt lonely but I had to steel myself and go on with life. This was my decision and I had to live with it.

Soon my life fell into a routine. I took care of my baby Nikki; I gave her this name after my late mother whose name was Nikanksha. I made myself hands-on mother and left the care of house, cooking and the garden to Tekka and Neema, they gave me no reason to complain and proved good companions in my loneliness.

Nikki was growing to be a fine healthy baby and she seldom cried or troubled anyone except when she was hungry. I was receiving regular calls from Reena from Delhi. As a physician Reena had a fairly successful private practice. She was married to Dr. Sadanand Kirki, who had been her class-mate in Medical College in Bangalore. They had got married after completing their postgraduate degrees and had one son, now eight years old, Vishu, a handsome boy with serious studious look.

Reena would bring me up to date on the latest happenings in Mumbai as she frequently visited the city in connection with various seminars and tell me interesting stories about the social scene in Delhi. I had not allowed news papers or television into my cottage. I wanted to have no connection with the world outside and distract me. Reena was my only link with the outside world.

After a month of my arrival in Dalhousie Reena called me as usual late at night. She sounded disturbed; her voice was shaky as she told me that Ashwin had suffered heart attack earlier in the day while he was attending the parliament session. He had been rushed to the hospital and a team of doctors was monitoring his health; his wife who was away in U.K, attending secretary level meeting was arriving by mid night. Reena was tearful as she disconnected the line.

I sat there holding the receiver in my hand. Deep down in my heart I felt a stirring; was I somehow, responsible for Ashwin's condition! Had my disappearance caused him distress! He was aware that I was carrying his child; I had told me so but also assured him that it would not cause any scandal for him or his family. "You can go on being a happily married family man with a successful political career" I had tried to sound calm, when I told him this.

My pregnancy had been confirmed by my doctor the same day as Ashwin had been given the ticket, second time to contest the election from Surnampur constituency for Lok Sabha. Owing to his close relationship with the party high command, he was seen as an important candidate. Fathering a love-child would finish his political career, I was aware of it and after a great deliberation with myself I had taken the decision that I will give birth to the child and face the flake. Reena my dearest friend and Ashwin's younger sister was aware of my condition. She had reasoned with me that birth of a child, will cause a great scandal for me also. After all I was a well known writer, a political journalist, whose views on politics and social issues were respected by all. I held a responsible job in a prestigious national news paper. My two books; one on political turmoil in Afghanistan and second, a plain fiction; a love story had been declared bestseller books. "The world is opening for you and you want to destroy this by your decision to have the baby!" Reena had pleaded with me, "Despite our veneer of broad mindedness, we are very conservative at heart. People in public life have to protect their image and have a halo around them. Think what your child will have to face. You know Radhika; she will not let Dada divorce her. She may not have given him a child in fifteen years of their married life, blaming him for it; she will raise hell if she ever comes to know about this child. Don't be an emotional fool Sukriti, Indian society is not ready yet to accept un wed mothers" Reena spoke to me at length and even cited examples of some girls she had known who were single mothers and the difficulty they had to face in bringing up their children alone.

I had read somewhere that even tinniest bird like wren fights with the owl to save its young ones in the nest. I wanted to fight with every ounce of my being for the tiny life growing inside me.

I had fallen in love and given myself wholly to this man. There were no promises made. Ashwin had never led me up the garden path or shown me any ray of hope that our relationship could ever have legal sanction. He had warned me at the outset of our relationship, "Sukriti, I cannot promise you legal relationship, because it is not in my hands, but I will love you as long as I am alive, my feelings, nobody can take away from me. I am aware and so must you be that our relationship may never have the social acceptability." For me his love was enough. I had never been very demanding. I would have been foolish to ever harbor any such hope. I had got into this relation with my eyes open.

CHAPTER 2

The salubrious climate, the peace of Dalhousie did much to assuage my feelings. I took to gardening and writing. All my spare time away from Nikki was spent in either tending to the little garden at the back of the cottage or reading and writing. Within one year of my arrival in Dalhousie I had finished writing two novels. The theme of one of them was love affair between a hard core terrorist and a simple village girl set against the backdrop of Himachal Pradesh in Chamba, the beautiful district of which Dalhousie town forms a part. Another novel was based on the theme of political uncertainty in the state of Jammu and Kashmir due to raging secessionist movement and its effect on the lives of those couples who had dared to break the social taboo against inter-religious marriages. One such couple was the Kashmiri pundit girl, Dr. Rajeshwari Tikko, who had married Dr Javed Ashraf; a Muslim doctor. The novel recounted the turmoil their marriage caused in the valley, the social and political backlash it brought. How they survived it all and they had hardly settled into a peaceful married life when Kashmir valley was ablaze by the terrorism led from across the border.

It was also around this time that I started writing my thoughts and the events of my life in my diary. Whenever I had time on my hands, I would pen my thoughts in my diary. It became my inseparable companion and catharsis for my pent up feelings. I would pour out my heart in its pages, sometimes smudging its papers with my tears. Loneliness is the biggest sufferance of a human being.

I had sent the soft copies of my books to my publisher in Delhi and the books were well received. Reena told me that with the appearance of these books in the market, the media had restarted tracing my whereabouts. There were different versions floated by the media; one was that I had migrated to USA; another had declared that I had married some rich NRI and was living in Norway and one media house had almost come closer to the truth that I was living in some part in North India with my child The success of my books aroused people's interest in my life again. Some praised my courage in bringing my love child into this world while others thought that celebrities were role models for youth and their unconventional life style was tarnishing the institution of marriage.

Reena of course; the ever-gentle sensitive person narrated these to me in the mildest possible terms. How like her, to be so thoughtful as not to hurt others feelings! I was told that Ashwin's wife would often taunt Reena about me, whenever they happened to meet at family gatherings. Once when Reena had gone to meet her mother, she had met Radhika and Ashwin there. Radhika had commented about one of my books that she found in the book store and asked Reena if she was still in contact with me. Reena had feigned ignorance about my whereabouts. Radhika had remarked contemptuously "Your friend Sukriti, was a bold one! Can you imagine holding a press conference to announce shamelessly that she was carrying a child! I wonder why she did not disclose the name of the father of her child, what fun it would have been to know the identity of her lover!" Ashwin, sitting across the room talking to his mother had looked up sharply at his wife, his face turning red but he said nothing and left the room on the pretext of making some important calls from his room.

Reena told me that later that night when Reena was about to leave for airport to catch her flight to Mumbai, Ashwin had insisted on driving her to the airport himself. Her husband was in London attending some medical conference. On the way Ashwin was silent and lost in his thoughts and Reena could see that he was disturbed. Ashwin stopped the car as they were nearing the airport and turned to look at Reena, "Will you answer me truthfully if I asked you about Sukriti" Ashwin questioned her. "Yes Dada, tell me what do you want to know?" Reena had said.

"I will not ask you where she is because if I know her whereabouts I will not be able to restrain myself from going there. I have promised her that I will not come to her, unless she wants me to, but how is the baby?" Ashwin continued. "I had come to know from Sadanand that she had given birth to our daughter in Breach Candy Hospital. Beyond that he did not divulge anything. Reena please tell me how is she, how is my baby? I am always thinking of both, wondering why I am suffering. I have become a father, I have child but I cannot see my child, nor give my name to her". Ashwin's voice had trailed in emotions and Reena told me that his eyes were filled with tears.

"Dada time is the best healer, leave everything to God. He will find some way" Reena had consoled Ashwin.

I listened to this information but made no comment. It was my fault. I had not given time to Ashwin to take a decision. I had apprehensions of public outcry; a prominent political figure involved in extra-marital relations with a well-known journalist and writer, his wife's reaction; her humiliation; his family's reputation; how could he leave all these! From the very beginning of our relationship, I was aware that our relationship had no future. There was no way it would have permanent footing. Yet there was an irresistible force that had drawn us together. We had both fought against our desires, tried to be indifferent to each other. I had even taken an overseas position to get out of his way. Perhaps out of sight may push him out of my mind, I had thought. However, when two people are destined to fall in a relationship the fates contrive to bring them together.

My first encounter with Ashwin Solanki was under odd circumstances. Being a theatre buff in my free time I used to act in plays, directed by my dear friend Nakul Sharma of National School of Drama during a theater fest being organized by the famous theatre club of Mumbai; 'Kalakaar' a play based on Sharat Chandra Chatopadhya's novel 'Devdas' was being staged. I had taken a week off from my newspaper job to play the part of 'Chandramukhi', the courtesan who falls in love with Devdas. The fest was to be inaugurated by the young minister, Ashwin Solanki, the minister of state for cultural affairs at center. He had been earlier an IAS officer but due to his close relationship with the president of the Prajya Party, the ruling party in the country, he was asked to resign from the Administrative Service and contest the election from the Parliamentary Constituency, Surnampur district. The close confidante of the President of Prajya Party, Sampuran Mukul, had earlier held this seat but his sudden death, due to cardiac failure had created the vacancy. The newspapers were filled with the reports of the young IAS officer Ashwin Solanki, who was making his political debut in the by-election. It was also said that he was not keen to join politics but out of respect for his maternal uncle, the president of the ruling Party, he had agreed. He was an alumnus of St. Xavier's Mumbai and completed his MBA from Stanford University USA. He had preferred administrative services over many career options he had in multi-national companies. Ashwin was married to an Indian Foreign Service diplomat, who was at that time posted at Sweden. They had no children and one of the gossip columns had hinted at long distance marriage gone sour.

Ashwin had won the elections against his rival of the Kranti Party. He had been inducted into the council of ministers as the minister of state for cultural affairs. It was often whispered in the corridors of power that he was slated to play an important part in the party affairs and the government. Praised for his deft handling of the media, he was often invited for panel discussions on the television and was seen as a great votary of freedom of speech Ashwni Solanki was a versatile man; a weekly columnist on foreign affairs in a leading English national daily, his views were greatly appreciated by the readers. He was also a member of the young Parliamentarians Cricket Club and played as medium pace bowler. Ashwin Solanki had also warmed himself to the social circuit of New Delhi and his pictures were often splashed on Page Three of the glossy newspapers. One could call him a man with high pedigree, great education, and professional success; he had it all.

At the inaugural ceremony, Ashwin Solanki lighted the inaugural lamp and gave an impressive speech on the importance of encouraging fine arts. He spoke briefly but in measured tones and stayed to watch the first play. It was my play Devdas and I played my part with my usual verve and nuances. At the end of the play all artists were briefly introduced to Ashwin Solanki. He seemed amused when he was told that I was a full time journalist for the popular newspaper. He told me that he had read some of my articles and found my style of writing 'interesting'. He left immediately as he had to take a flight back to Delhi to attend the Parliament Session in the evening.

When one is young time seems to gallop and before I could realize one year had passed after my meeting Ashwin Solanki. I was now the political analyst of my newspaper. It was no doubt, an important position, where I had to be abreast of all happenings, be they government policies, cabinet decisions, meetings, Parliamentary proceedings, policy matters. I had to give analysis of the political affairs and their effect on the country. Since our newspaper had the policy to remain impartial to political parties, there were many occasions when my views were critical of the ruling party. In my new position I had to meet the politicians, parliamentarians, and ministers to know about the new policies they had framed with regard to their departments and their stand against the criticism of the opposition parties and on the current political issues.

Once a sting operation was conducted by a particular electronic media on a central government minister and shown him accepting a huge cache of money for some quid-pro-quo. This exposure put the ruling party in an awkward position. Although the minster was dropped from the council of ministers, soon enough the damage had been done to the image of the party. The scam continued to rock the parliament for many days. Ashwin Solanki, known for his warm relation with media was chosen by his party for fire fighting. In the mean time the ruling party had issued a gag order on its leaders about talking to the media, whatever stand the party was to take, will be made known at the due time by its spokesperson ; these were the orders of the party president. In this regard Ashwin held a press conference in Delhi to explain his party's stand. I had come from Mumbai to represent my newspaper; People's Voice. He handled the embarrassing questions of corruption in his party, the numerous scams exposed by media, very deftly. I was admiring this man's calmness and presence of mind as he tried to answer the volley of questions the reporters were flooding him with. When it was my turn, I stood up and introduced myself. I saw a flicker of recognition as he smiled encouragingly at me.

"Mr Solanki after the series of scams exposed by the media, it is reported that your government is bringing a bill to impose moral code of conduct on the media. Is it an indirect way of muzzling the media?" I questioned.

"Not at all, there is no such move, I am personally a great advocate of freedom of media, but they have to understand their responsibility as the fourth pillar of democracy and restrain themselves from sensationalism and character assassination" Ashwin Solinki said.

"You mean to say that exposing minister's misdeeds amounts to creating sensationalism and character assassination" I retorted. I could see he was smiling through hard-pressed lips but maintained his composure, "There have been many fabricated sting operations, when the people involved said something but their statements were blown out of proportion and twisted out of context to malign the government. This is the high handedness of media and they must understand their responsibility also. "Ashwin Solinki declared.

I said, "You are not being fair to the media, of late there have been many efforts by your government to suppress the free expression, recently your government blocked out some social networking sites on the pretext of anti national content posted on them". His secretary immediately took up the next question from a reporter of another newspaper. I was standing with my hand raised but Ashwin Solanki ignored me, which left me flustered and I sat down. During the meeting, I raised my hand several times to ask more questions but neither the minister nor his secretary looked in my direction. I was angry and started scribbling furiously on my note pad. I left the conference hall and went to the Delhi Bureau of my newspaper put my notes together to compose the report. Perhaps my anger at being ignored may have got the better of me I made the report a bit sarcastic, indirectly hinting that the minister's answers were prevarications; a cover up for his corrupt colleagues. Later that evening I flew back to Mumbai.

Next day I received a call from the personal secretary of Ashwin Solanki saying politely that the minister wanted to speak with me if I could spare some time. 'Ok please put him on the line' I said. I was expecting a reprimand or even a barb for my report but to my utter disbelief Mr Solanki's voice was dripping with honey "Miss Sukriti, I read your report, you sound very angry with me. Don't be". He said and after some pleasantries he disconnected. I wondered what was behind this, a threat, a warning or a good-natured remark!

After that I went hammer and tongs against some decisions the government had taken lately, called them beneficial to only certain section of the business community. I was especially critical of the functioning of the ministry headed by Ashwin Solanki calling the policies of his ministry as partisan. This went on for few weeks till my anger thawed a bit and then I forgot all about him.

CHAPTER 3

That year the summer was unbearable in Mumbai and I needed some break so I took leave for a week and decided to visit my maternal grandmother at Srinagar in Kashmir. It was nearly four years since I had visited her. She had become a mother to me after my mother's untimely death ten years ago. I had completed my degree in mass communication when my mother took ill, and despite the best available medical care and treatment she passed away. I was shattered, being the youngest of the two brothers and three sisters; I was very close to my mother. Both my brothers and sisters were married and well settled. My father had built a house in Delhi after his retirement from the central government job as an engineer but my brothers and sisters did not allow him to live alone in his house so he spent few months with my elder brother, sometimes he would stay with my sisters who lived in different parts of the country. At the moment he was living with my eldest sister in Kodaikanal. She was a doctor and married to a doctor.

My grandmother whom I fondly called Nanu was overjoyed to see me. She had a beautiful cottage at the foot hills of Shankracharya Hill, quite close to Dal Gate area in Srinagar. This house was surrounded by almond, Walnut and Cherry trees. As a child I had spent many happy hours under these trees collecting the fruit that had dropped from them. My grandmother was a matriarch who took care of the house and the fruit orchards situated in Fokker Village situated fifty kilometers from the city, all by herself and lived alone. Her two sons, my maternal uncles with their families had settled in the UK. They had tried to cajole Nanu to live with them but she had stubbornly refused to leave her home and live among strangers. My uncles had been so exasperated with her stubbornness that they not only stopped pleading with her but also stopped visiting her. Secretly my aunts were pleased to be away from her because Nanu could be quite a terror. She never complained but spent her time chatting with many old servants she had, living on her property at Dal Gate.

Out of all her grand children, she loved me the most. I was told by one of her old servants that when my mother had conceived me she was not mentally prepared to have the fifth child and wanted to abort the pregnancy. When Nanu had heard of this she was furious," No, Nikanksha, you will do no such thing", she had told my mother. Later on when I was born, a fifth child and that too a girl; my mother was disappointed. My father's younger brother had no child even after ten years of marriage so he was very keen to adopt me. My father loved his younger brother too much to refuse him. My parents might have agreed to give me in adoption had it not been for my grandmother. When she was told about this she told my parents categorically that she would keep me if they thought me to be a burden. She persuaded my parents to leave me with her in Kashmir. My mother thought that it would be good for my grandmother if she had something to occupy herself with her. Nanu had an old servant who had been my youngest uncle's maid; she looked look after me. I was about six months old when Nanu brought me to Srinagar and I spent ten years of my childhood with Nanu in Kashmir. Those were the happiest days of my life. Later on my parents took me with them to Delhi for better education in a public school.

This time also my stay in Kashmir was a pleasant one I visited some of my relatives and often went sightseeing on my own, just taking the twelve years girl of Nanu's maid servant with me to keep me company. Footloose and fancy free I went where my fancy took me, sometimes trekking the Hari Parbat Hill to pay my obeisance at the shrine situated on the hill, sometimes waking along the Boulevard Road. During one such trip I met Ashwin Solanki and his wife.

I was getting down the steps of Shalimar Garden when I saw three white Ambassador Cars, one bearing the national flag come to a halt at the entrance of the garden. From one of the cars a chauffeur came out and opened the back door. I saw the tall figure of Ashwin Solanki alighting from the car and followed by a lady in jeans and sweatshirt. He was dressed in white cotton kurta and pajama. He looked so different from what I had seen. He and his wife were escorted by four commandos as they came up the steps. I tried to move away to avoid coming face to face with him but he had seen me and recognized me "Hello Sukriti Kaul, what a surprise! Are you here on journalistic assignment?" He asked me.

"Hello Mr. Solanki, I am here on a holiday staying with my grandmother" I replied.

He introduced me to his wife. She was very beautiful and tall and wore her hair very short. We exchanged some perfunctory greetings and I was about to excuse myself on the pretext that "Grandma will be worried, I am already late". He insisted that I should accompany them into the garden. His wife told me that her husband had come to Kashmir on an official visit and she accompanied him to Kashmir. She told me rather shyly that they had visited this Mughal Garden on their honeymoon, many years back and she wanted to visit this place again. I listened quietly only nodding my head occasionally. The tourist department of Srinagar had arranged a small reception for the minister and his wife at the cafeteria in the garden. The minister insisted that I should also join them for the tea. I agreed reluctantly. I was getting bored listening to the conversation of the various people in the group. Tea over, I took my leave and got into my grandmother's gypsy jeep and drove away. This gypsy was my grandmother's favorite vehicle and whenever she visited her farm outside the city she asked her driver to take her in this jeep.

I had another encounter with Ashwin Solanki during my stay in Srinagar. It was at the wedding reception of the local politician Mr. Taibu-din's son. Mr Taibu-din was the General Secretary of the J & K unit of Prajya Party and known to be an astute politician. He had known my grandfather's family since four decades and often visited Nanu' to inquire about her welfare. My grandmother avoided such functions; therefore she insisted that I should attend the marriage reception and take some gift on her behalf. I did not want to disappoint her and went to the reception. It was while I was congratulating the newly married couple standing, on the dais made for this occasion, I heard someone say 'the minister has come' I took a few steps backwards to make room for other guests and nearly collided with Ashwin Solanki climbing up the step of the dais. I would have fallen on him he had not stretched his arm to prevent the fall. I apologized for my haste but he silenced me with his smile. I quickly got down from the dais and went into the farther corner of the reception hall and sat down. I saw that Ashwin Solanki was alone except for the two commandos standing behind him. He was wearing a dark colored bandgala coat and dark trousers, looking more like a film star than a minister.

I could have a good look from my place all around. I knew some friends of my grandmother the rest were all strangers to me. I was undecided whether I should stay little more or make my exit, when I saw from the corners of my eye Ashwin Solanki coming towards me followed by the host. I stood up to greet them. He pulled a chair before his host could pull one for him. He sat down a few feet away from me and politely urged his host not to bother about him as he was comfortable there. The host went away reluctantly to attend to other guests. Ashwin Solanki sat quietly I was getting painfully conscious of his presence. He was looking around casually and I sat their immobile wondering whether I should say something to break the silence. I turned my head to look at him and found him looking at me. He looked away.

I asked more out of politeness than any interest, "Mr Solanki are you going to be here for few more days?"

"No, I will be leaving tomorrow morning, Mrs Solanki has already left in the afternoon for Delhi' he answered".

"Oh!" was all I could muster and again silence.

This time Ashwin said something that took me by surprise "Miss Sukriti I am intrigued by you, an independent lady, gifted with wonderful power of the pen who can act as beautifully as she can write".

I turned all shades of pink by his remark and smiled gently, "I am just an ordinary girl, who thinks she has to stand on her own in the male dominated society".

"You are so self-assured, so tough, yet so feminine, it would be interesting to know you better' Ashwin Solanki said enigmatically and got up, his guards quickly took their position behind him. He smiled and with a wave of his hand moved away. I kept looking at his retreating back, thinking of his remarks.

Later at night, I was putting my cell phone on charging when there was SMS ring on it, I thought it must me some joke my colleagues often sent me, so I took out my reading glasses to read. It read, "Thinking of you" and was signed as A.S. It took me sometime to decipher the puzzling abbreviation, but why Ashwani Solanki would send me a message like this and where did he get my number from. I even tried the childhood way of counting sheep to fall asleep but I could not sleep. My mind was racing. Ashwin Solanki found me intriguing but I was just like any other career girl. Was he trying to flirt with me or was he just passing his time!

Next day my grandmother had to visit one of her orchards where her tenants were having some problems with the neighboring farm owner and police had to be called in and they had arrested two of her most trustworthy farms-hands. My grandmother left early in the morning with her driver Razaak and was not expected to return before nightfall. I decided to spend the day by cleaning my grandmother's wardrobes and clear the clutter from her room. Dressed in jeans and tee-shirt, I tied my long hair in a loose bun and sat down to organize her things. Nanu had so many saris of all varieties and mostly in pastel shades with every sari she had matching shawl. I liked her taste. I was so busy putting her saris on the hangers along with matching blouse and petticoats, music player was on and a beautiful old song from a Hindi film was playing, I did not realize that there was knocking at the gate. My grandmother lived in a house that was as big as a mansion with a tall wooden gate that had a heavy iron handle. Nanu was old fashioned about door bells and preferred the old way of knocking with handle. It was only after sometime I heard the knocking. Who could it be! Tahera my Nanu's maid had gone with Nanu. Rashid her husband had gone to the market to buy trout fish another favorite of my grandmother. I went hurriedly to the gate and through the chink peeped out and to my utter amazement I found Ashwin Solanki standing with a large hat falling over his forehead. How did he get my address! What on earth is he doing here!. I quickly opened the gate, my heart beating against my ribs. I greeted him uneasily. He looked at me hard and preceded me into our open lawn and then into the glass room which was actually our old veranda that my grandfather had had covered with glass to have some warmth in the winter. I walked quietly behind this tall man. He was all alone. He entered the room and turned to have a good look at me, "Are you surprised? Oh! That is an understatement you are dismayed to see me, but I had to come to meet you. I got your address from Taibu-din, I had to be very tactful in getting the address, he could put two and two together and cook some colorful story about you and me. So here I am". Ashwin Solanki spoke with a serious face.

"You could have called me, is there something you wish to discuss with me." I said trying as best as I could to keep my voice calm, though I was feeling nervous in his presence.

He looked at me said nothing and kept looking at me.

"Please set down, I will get some water, my grandmother has gone to her farm and the servants are also not here". I went on without realizing that I had clutched the curtain in my hand and was holding on to it for my dear life.

Ashwin again did not say anything but he took the seat near the window. I quickly went into the kitchen which was at the back of the house. In my hurry to escape from his presence, I was walking briskly. Nanu had recently had the wooden floor of the dining room polished and it had become slippery. Tahera had already slipped on this, twice. I was wearing rubber slippers which had worn out at the soles; one of grandmother's old pairs. I slipped and lost my balance, trying to steady myself I grabbed at the thick silk curtain of the door. This must have exerted a lot of pressure on the heavy wooden pelmet; it came crashing on my head. All I could feel was a something heavy falling on my head an excruciating pain and then blackout.

When I opened my eyes, I found myself on my bed and a wet cold towel pressed on my head and Ashwin Solanki was sitting close to me on the bed holding the wet towel to my head. My head was splitting with pain, I tried to sit up but he held my shoulders and kept me in a lying position pressing my shoulder and gently touching my head. He was touching my neck, my ears to see if I had hurt any other part of my body. He looked so caring and there was so much concern in his voice, when he spoke to me that I was touched. I tried to say something but the throbbing in my head made my words incoherent. He brought his lips close to my ears and whispered, "Sukriti are you ok, tell me, I will take you to the hospital?" His voice was soft like a caress on my ears.

"I am ok, but my head is splitting. I am feeling nauseous", I said weekly and the next moment I was throwing up all over the floor, retching miserably and also crying. He put his arms around me and held me tightly against his chest as I gasped for breath. After sometime when my gasping had ceased, he made me drink some water. I obeyed him like a child. He put me down on the bed and went towards the dressing table drawer, he took out wet tissue papers and towel and began to sponge my face and neck. He asked me where I kept my fresh clothes, weakly I pointed towards the wooden cupboard. He took out a caftan and asked me to gently lift my head. I was too weak to argue, I did what I was told. He removed my tee-shirt, wiped my bosom with the wet tissues, I was feeling too embarrassed, but his movements were clinical. He put the caftan over my head and then lifted me in his arms as if I did not weigh anything; he made me sit in the lounge chair kept in the middle of my room "where do you keep the linen?" He asked me. I pointed towards the cupboard. He brought out a fresh pair of bed sheets and pillows covers and removed the soiled ones. I watched him through my half closed eyes as he spread out the bed sheets and put the pillow covers. He then carried me back to the bed and sat there for a long time touching my head. He said nothing but urged me to close my eyes. I drifted into a sound sleep.

God knows I long I must have slept because when I awoke, it was evening time and I heard voices coming from the dining room. It was Rashid and I heard Ashwin talking. I called out to Rashid, who came running into my room looking very frightened, I assured him that I was alright. He suggested that he should call Nanu's family doctor, I told him that I was much better and it was just a little lump on my head that was hurting. Ashwin Solanki also came into my room. He looked tired; his hair was falling over his forehead. In that condition also I could not help admiring him. He looked so much at home in my Nanu's house as if he belonged here. He asked Rashid to prepare chicken soup for me and Rashid respectfully went out of the room. Ashwin sat on my bed and put his hand on my head as if it was the most natural thing to do. Why I was not feeling self-conscious; could it be my accident that had made me so brazen that I did not mind a stranger touching so intimately! He kept stroking my head; there was strange expression in his eyes. Rashid appeared after sometime with two bowls of soup and some toasts. He left it on the table near my bed and went out quietly.

Ashwin fed me soup with his own hands as I lay propped up against the pillows. He urged me to have a toast which I did. We were like two old companions doing the most usual things. Later on he pulled the blanket over me and tucked me under the bed sheets and kept stroking my head gently till I felt drowsy again. I remember that before falling asleep, I had felt his lips close to my temple. Was he going to kiss me! I have no clear idea. I heard him whisper something in my ears, but I cannot recall what it was.

When I wake up next it was late in the night and Nanu had returned. Rashid must have told her about my accident, he had not been able to recognize Ashwin. All he could tell Nanu was that I had a visitor from Delhi and while I was going to bring some water for him, I had slipped and fainted and when Rashid had returned from the market, he was horrified to see me lying immobile on my bed and the 'Sahib' from Delhi was sitting on the chair near my bed talking to some body on the phone. 'Sahaib' had introduced himself as 'Sukriti Didi's friend and he asked me to bring some medicine and didi was lying half unconscious" Rashid narrated the story to Nanu.

Nanu was worried; she insisted that I should see a physician. "What if there is a concussion!" she said: I would not hear of it, as a matter of fact I was feeling much better but too groggy to stand on my feet.

Next morning I saw two SMS on my cell phone both from Ashwin Solanki 'you gave me fright of my life, hope the pain has subsided!' Second message read "you looked so relaxed, peaceful, lying in bed, did not have the heart to disturb you, get well soon".

I was touched by these two messages; they appeared so caring as if we had known each other for a long time. This incident had brought us closer, even though only for a few hours that he had held me in his arms and I had felt so much at peace. What was it that had drawn us to each other! Was it just lust; physical attraction between a hot blooded man and young woman! Ashwin Solanki was in my thoughts for many hours. I had to drag my mind away from his thoughts and remind myself that he after all he was a happily married man, why would he have any interest in me!

In the afternoon I received another message from him 'leaving for Delhi, wanted to meet you, but I must not be reckless'. What does he mean by 'reckless!' perhaps he had to think of his position also I concluded.

I had a few more days left of my vacation but I was now restless and needed to get back to my work. Nanu was disappointed when I told her that I had planned to leave next day and my plane ticket had been booked. Before my departure Nanu gave me some pieces of his antique jewellery saying "I may not be alive when you get married, take these and wear them on your wedding day ".Parting from Nanu has always been painful to me, this time also it was the same I could see that she was lonely and needed me to be with her.

I left for Mumbai; the land of my calling. My headache persisted and I had to take painkillers to deaden the pain. I saw my physician who subjected me to many tests and finally declared that there was a little swelling on my skull which would subside with medicine. There was so much work piled on my desk that I forget all about my physical discomfiture or my experience at Srinagar. I spent nearly eighteen hours at the office, writing articles, analyzing political events, once in while I would see Ashwin Solanki on the TV attending a discussion. I would look at him; remember that day in Srinagar and often wonder about the incoherent words he had whispered in my ears that afternoon. "Sukriti you are imaging things". I would gently admonish myself and laugh aloud.

CHAPTER 4

Few months after my return to Mumbai, my editor sent me on an overseas assignment to Angola to cover the ongoing civil war there. I witnessed terrible scenes; the malnourished children and the women being raped by the outlaws, the loot and the general lawlessness in the country. Certain areas in Angola were considered too risky for the foreign press to venture into. We could only go with the army escorts to the down town areas of Angola, to shoot the events or speak to the local people or govt. officials.

I was accompanied on this assignment by my old friend, Vishwas Shaw, who was our ace photographer, and his assistant Satish Kochhar. Our movements were restricted. The entire foreign press representatives were lodged in Imperial Hotel, situated in the heart of Angola. This was considered to be the safest shelter and heavily guarded by army men. From here we would go in groups to different parts of the strife-torn areas where exchange of fire and bombing was a regular feature. The press and electronic media was covering every event and dispatching the videos and text messages at a great risk to their respective media.

One of the correspondents of a French newspaper Mariana François had become my great friend. She was seven months pregnant with her live-in partner; a doctor, who worked in the government hospital in France. She had not informed her employer about her pregnancy, fearing that they would not send her on this assignment. Mariana, Vishwas and I would often go together to collect information about the events taking place in the country. The government forces were becoming weak day by day as the rebel militia was consolidating its position. We all knew that it was just a matter of a few weeks when they would have complete control over the capital.

One day while we were covering the public address of the chief of their armed forces, a powerful explosion was heard close to the press stand. The bomb was so powerful that I fell few feet away from where I was standing, taking down notes. Mariana was standing in the corner of the press stand, there were screams, cries and people were running helter-skelter.

I could see through the screen of thick smoke the human flesh falling around, there was blood everywhere. My first thought was for my colleagues Vishwas and Satish; I stood up where I had fallen and began to look frantically around for them. I saw Satish with his torn and blood stained clothes lying on the floor, I ran towards him, he was alive but his back badly torn by the splinters. Vishwas was nowhere to be seen. There were dead bodies, people with torn limbs, broken skulls lying all over. The worst hit was the press stand. It was here that the bomb had been planted. I helped Satish to his feet and literally carried him to one side and put him down on the pavement under a tree. My worst fear was for Vishwas and Mariana. Where were they? The Ambulances of Red Cross Society and the government hospitals arrived at the scene immediately. I showed my press card to the officials doing the rescue work and had Satish sent in one of the ambulances to the Government medical centre. I promised him that I will join him shortly but I must find Vishwas and Mariana. I was frantically looking for them, turning the dead bodies over to see if my friends were there. I saw the torn body of one of the British Journalists; I had shared a drink with him only the previous day. He had told me that after this assignment he had planned to get married to his school time sweet heart who was training to be a nurse. Left side of his body had completely been blown away.

The army was helping to clear the dead and shift the wounded to the hospitals. I looked among the heap of dead bodies but I could not find any trace of Vishwas and Mariana. It was only after sometime that too with the help of army men that I was able to locate Vishwas who had fallen in the stampede and lost his consciousness. He was still unconscious when we found him, he was immediately put on the stretcher, few feet away from him lay Mariana her face bleeding the splinters of the bomb had pierced her face and chest. I could see there was blood trickling down her legs as she lay on her side unconscious, "Oh! My God," I remembered her pregnancy she was breathing hard, as if gasping for breath. The medics took her along with Vishwas to the hospital. I sat with them in the ambulance holding their hands and weeping.

In the hospital, Satish was immediately operated upon to remove the splinters form his shoulders and back. He had had narrow escape that the splinters had not hit him in the front. I was told that Mariana's condition was critical; she had lost a lot of blood, a splinter had ruptured her spleen. There was an apprehension that she may also lose her baby. The doctor told me that they would have to perform a caesarian section to save the baby and operate upon her spleen to take out the splinter. I was too numb with the horror of violence and death I had witnessed to think clearly. God knows how long I must have sat there. It was the sight of nurses that brought me back to my senses.

Mariana was operated upon to take out the premature baby. It was a tiny boy, he was immediately put into the incubator, and Mariana underwent a second operation, but due to profuse bleeding, she breathed her last on the operation table. The news shattered me. My first thought was towards the newborn; will he survive! I cried hysterically as Mariana's body was brought out from the operation theater. I held her cold lifeless hand promising to look after her child; I went on and on rambling till a doctor pulled me away. Later I was given a sleeping injection to put me to sleep.

I woke up at mid night, fully alert and began to search for Vishwas and Satish, the doctor on duty informed me that they were both out of danger and being kept in ICU and I should not worry about them. I met Mariana's Italian assistant, Santiana sitting on the bench, he told me that Mariana's body was in the morgue and her family has been informed. The French embassy officials would be coming any moment to take her body, to send it to her country. About the baby, there were some legal complications, as her employers were not told anything about her pregnancy. Her partner was informed and he would be here in two days to claim the baby. Santiana and I both hugged each other and cried bitterly.

This was the terrible side of the civil war. Why the militants had targeted the press, perhaps to warn the international community not to help the government. I sat with Santiana for the whole night sometimes weeping, or talking about the friends we had lost. In between, I also went to check on Vishwas and Satish, they were sleeping with numerous pipes inserted into their bodies both were young, strong and would probably remember this as a great adventure in their life but Mariana; her baby, 'Oh God' I sat down on the bench and cried bitterly.

The hospital was filled with people, officials of different embassies looking for their press representatives. I felt a touch on my shoulder and I turned my tear stained eyes to see an Indian official standing there. He introduced himself as Brigadier Mahvir Singh, Military Attaché in the Indian embassy in Angola. The Indian embassy had sent him to trace out the Indian media representatives. He had found out that two reporters of People's Voice Press had been injured. He already knew about Vishwas and Satish, and had also visited them in the ICU but it was me he had been searching for "Miss Kaul we have been searching you since the blast, our embassy is flooded by the calls for your safety from New Delhi ".

I looked at him without answering. "We have been asked by the ambassador to locate you and request you to get in touch with Mr. Solanki, the union minister". He said that Mr. Solanki has been promoted as the union minister. I wondered how long have I been out of the country to know all these happenings!

I remembered that I had no mobile on me perhaps in that turmoil it may have fallen somewhere. Brigadier Mahavir Singh gave me his mobile to speak. In fact he dialed the number himself. On the other end I heard Ashwin Solanki's voice, a kind of tremor in his voice when I said "hello", he said "Thank God Sukriti you are well. I have been besides myself with worry, when I heard the news, I thought I . . . . you were . . ." he did not complete the sentence. I could hear him trying to control his emotions.

"Don't worry Mr. Solanki, we are safe although, a bit shaken" I tried to sound casual. "Sukriti, I am reaching Angola tomorrow by afternoon in a special plane. Our government was sending the minister of state for foreign affairs to bring all our media representatives back but I requested the PMO to send me. I need to see you. I am coming" and then he disconnected.

Brigadier. Mahvir Singh urged me to return to the hotel and have rest. The doctors told me that my colleagues were out of danger and Mariana's baby was in good hands. I accompanied the Brig to the hotel and straight away went to my room. I was too afraid to ask the receptionist who had returned and who had not.

I had a fitful sleep, there were so many things playing on my mind, and the upper most was Mariana and her baby.

Next day I went to the hospital to check on Vishwas and Satish, they were weak but in good spirits, I joked a little and then the doctor told me to let them rest. I went in to the nursery to see Mariana's baby. The nurse showed a little creature with a tag around his wrist through, the glass walls. I thought he looked so much like Mariana, but being premature his features were not too distinct. The doctor informed me that luckily he was not hurt but being under weight and pre mature there was always danger of catching infection.

I offered a silent prayer for his recovery and went back to the hotel. I spent a few hours typing out the press briefs, selecting the pictures and sent the mail to my editor, to my brothers and sister informing them about my well-being. After that I must have fallen asleep because I woke up to the ringing of the intercom, it was the receptionist telling that I had a visitor. I said half-sleepily to show him in. I dozed off again.

A knock at the door woke fully me up and I went to open the door. It was Ashwin Solanki standing wearing a pair of blue jeans and white shirt, he was alone. As the door closed behind him he pulled me in his arms and held me tightly, murmuring my name, I was too dazed to speak, repeating my name again and again speaking endearments, touching my nose, my eyes, my lips with his hands as if to make sure that it was me and not my ghost. The terrible incident had made me quite vulnerable, finding a familiar face from my country so over powered me that I began to cry and clung to him. He kissed my cheeks, and then my lips. I became completely reckless and I returned his kisses with an equal ardor, crying out his name, telling him to hold me and not let me go. Tears trickling down my cheeks. He held me for a long time in his arms, stroking my hair, my back saying repeatedly "My darling, my darling, I thought, I had lost you".

I shuddered and told him what I had been through "Hush, my darlings don't think about it and now no more of these assignments". He said his voice soft with concern. He lifted me and put me gently on the bed and cuddled me in his arms. We sat like this for a long time no words were needed just holding each other and hearing our heart beats. We could communicate our feelings to each other.

The ringing of his cell phone disturbed our blissful moment. He took it out of his pocket to see the number and his face became serious. He answered the call speaking in monosyllables 'yes or 'no' 'ok', "I will return soon". I could hear the voice of a woman on the other end. It must be his wife, I thought and with this thought I shrunk and moved away from him. If he noticed this he did not comment but his tone became formal and distant, "Government has sent a plane to take away all the media members. You will leave with them; your wounded colleagues will also be flown in the same plane under medical supervision. Be ready by 6am in the morning. An army vehicle will come to pick you from this hotel". He said.

"Yes I will be ready' I answered and stood up. He understood my gesture and stood up from the bed and I moved towards the door to open it for him. He walked towards me, stopped as if he wanted to say something but he said nothing. For a long time he stood at the door looking at me and then he was gone.

After he left I switched on the TV to hear the local news. The thought of Mariana and her baby kept haunting me as they were showing the horrifying images of the bomb blast. It was then that I decided that I will stay behind to wait for Mariana's partner to come and once the baby was in his care, I would return.

Later in the evening, I asked for a cab and went to see my colleagues and Mariana's baby. Vishwas was appearing cheerful because he had come to know that he was flying home the next morning. Satish was still under the effect of medicine to comprehend what was happening. I went into the children's ward and requested the nurse to take me to the nursery. She recognized me and took me to Mariana's baby. The baby was getting stronger, she informed me on the way. It is often seen that twenty eight weeks old baby can survive and there was greater chance that the infant will pull through but he will have to stay in the incubator for at least two weeks.

The nurses had already started feeding him few ounces of milk through a dropper. I looked at the baby through the glass pane; he was awake and kicking with his legs. Although very tiny, he looked stronger. I stood there for a long time praying for peace for Mariana's soul and happy for the life of her baby. I asked for permission of the hospital authorities to visit her body in morgue, her body was being flown to France by a special plane late that night. Walking through the long corridor of the morgue, I was thinking it could have been me there, why could not I have died in her place; at least her child would not have become motherless at birth. I must have spoken my thoughts aloud because the morgue attendant, an elderly man gently patted me on my back as if to console me. Marian's beautiful face had turned pale, her body looked very small. I could not stand there anymore and walked out my vision blurred with tears.

I returned to the ICU to have a long chat with Vishwas, I explained to him why I need to stay behind. Telling him all about Mariana's death, the child birth, he was terribly moved and sobbed like a baby. We sat together for a long time, when I bid him good-bye and kissed him gently on his forehead, the poor boy clung to me, he had seen so much pain to last him a lifetime.

After leaving the hospital, I took a cab and asked the driver to drive me to French embassy. I wanted to know if they had any news as to when Mariana's partner was arriving, they told me that he was due to arrive three days after because he wanted to attend Mariana's burial, which means it will be another four to five days stay in Angola for me. I was determined to stay even at the risk to my life and personally see the baby being handed over to his father.

The government had warned the international media personnel not to move around unescorted in the city and here I was travelling all alone with a stranger, the cab driver but he seemed an elderly man and spoke broken English. I felt very secure with him. I asked him if he could tell me about an inexpensive hotel, which was safe, and where I could stay, I explained to him the reason for my staying behind. He was moved by my story and promised to help me out.

The same night we found a decent hotel and with the help of the driver I checked out of the Imperial Hotel. I left a message for the Indian Embassy officials explaining the reason for prolonging my stay.

This hotel was actually a Guest House run by an elderly couple. They had converted the outhouse of their cottage into a comfortable guesthouse. They welcomed me and when the driver explained to them my situation they were very touched. I was looked after by them very well. The driver promised to drive me around, when I tried to tip him, he refused saying "you our guest, no, money".

The army vehicle had come at the appointed hour to pick the Indian media personnel and take them to the airport. Receptionist at the hotel had given them my letter. Vishwas told me later, on my arrival in India, that Mr Solanki was personally present at the airport to see off the Indian Media. He was looking around for someone. He sent the embassy staff to find out where I was. Vishwas told him that I had stayed behind to see Mariana's baby, "Mr. Solanki looked very angry and then drove away in the waiting car".

Yes, Ashwin had been furious, very angry. He had tried to contact me, but since I had lost my mobile at the site of bomb blast, I had not had time to get myself a new cell phone. The deputy counselor of the Indian Embassy was soon knocking at my door the same day in the evening. He explained that I was taking a great risk by living out of protected zone and that I should return by the next flight. He also told me 'Minister Sahib is very angry and has asked to put you on the next flight to India".

I told him of my moral responsibility towards Mariana's baby; whether he understood me or not but he left and nobody visited me again for the rest of my stay. I was at the hospital the whole day sitting outside the nursery, looking at the baby. The more I saw him the closer I felt to him, as if it was my baby lying in the incubator. The nurses were looking after him well and he was gaining weight. Looking at him I was constantly reminded of Mariana. In a few days that we had spent together, I had come to like her and now some invisible bond was pulling me towards her baby.

Eventually Mariana's partner arrived in Angola on the sixth day of the bomb blast. He drove straight to the hospital; I was setting outside the nursery, my eyes fixed on the baby, happily flaying his arms and kicking. He was accompanied by the hospital administrator and French embassy official. The hospital administrator recognized me and introduced me to the young man. His name was Oliver Chavez, he was around thirty years. I could see the expression of grief writ large on his face. He had long stubble growing, there were dark circles around his eyes. The administrator introduced me and told him why I was there. His voice choked with emotions as he thanked me for the concern for his son. He looked at his baby from the glass pane and tears began to roll down his cheeks. I went out as I did not want to cry and make a fool of myself.

After two hours he emerged from the nursery wing, I was sitting on the bench recalling the horror of past days. He sat next to me. It was a companionable silence, when words were not needed to tell how raw our grief was. He told me that he and Mariana were childhood sweet hearts and they had wanted to get married after Mariana had completed her foreign assignment. They were both excited about the baby and had planned to migrate to Landon where Mariana was hoping to join some media house.

There were so many memories. I sat in silence listening to his reminiscing. No words could have soothed his bleeding heart so I said nothing. Oliver was planning to return to France the next day but the doctor had told him that the baby needed to be kept in incubator for few days so he will have to stay back. I assured him that I will also stay back until the baby was fit to be taken out of the hospital. We spent many hours talking and taking long walks in the hospital lawns. Olive was worried about baby's health. He told me that he had very caring parents who had assured him that they would take care of his son. He had promised himself that he would dedicate his life to his son. I rather liked Oliver. He was very polite, very emotional, a typical Frenchman. He had a good medical practice as a physician back home. Mariana's old parents had been shattered by her death since she was the only child. They were in a state of deep shock; perhaps the baby will bring back some cheer in their lives, Oliver hoped. He was staying in a hotel near the hospital. Sitting outside the nursery or walking I was most of the time with him. Oliver wanted to know the manner in which Mariana had died; it was too ghastly to tell this young man so I made up some story about Mariana falling and hurting herself in the stampede that followed the blast. I don't know whether he believed my story but he did not ask again.

On the eve of his departure Oliver made me, promise that I will keep in touch with him and become the godmother of his son. He named the baby Mark because of the similar letters of Mariana's name. We dined together and the cab driver drove us around the city. Oliver wanted to visit the spot where Mariana had been hit. We drove there and for a long time we stood at a corner looking at the spot, where we could still see the bloodstains. The police had cordoned off the entire area; we came back to the hospital.

In the evening, Mark was handed over to his father in the presence of the French Embassy official, after completing many legal formalities. Oliver was worried that the baby was too small for him to take care alone. I assured him that I will keep the baby with me for the night until the nurse, whom the embassy had appointed to accompany Oliver and Mark to France, arrived in the morning.

I took the baby with me holding it for the first time in my arms. He felt so warm. The owners of my guest house were so overjoyed to see the baby. They helped me to change his clothes and feed him through the dropper. He slept peacefully throughout the night. I kept a strict vigil over him, not sleeping a wink lest Mark should wake up or want feeding. Next morning Oliver was brought by my cab driver friend to my guest house. We had a good breakfast and drove to the airport. Mark was all the while sleeping peacefully in my arms. At the airport the embassy officials were waiting with French nurse who immediately took charge of Mark like an efficient nurse. Parting was as painful for me as it was for Oliver. In last two weeks, we had become good friends sharing our fears, aspirations, and love for little Mark. He hugged me affectionately and I bent down to kiss little Mark as I touched his cheek he opened his eyes and smiled. I still remember his smile through the half-closed eyes, "love you baby. God bless you" I said and watched them move away towards the tarmac. I felt lonely and bereft of everything. I sat down for sometime but my driver friend told me that I too had to catch my flight in few minutes time. Saying a fond good bye to my friend I collected my boarding pass. In one day I had parted from three dear friends not sure whether I will meet them again.

CHAPTER 5

I arrived in Delhi unannounced and did not want to meet anyone. The past few days had drained me physically and emotionally. I did not want to visit my family. I called up my close friend Aayesha, who was unmarried like me, teaching in a college, Aayesha was liberated in her views and non-interfering kinds. She invited me to come and stay with her promising me that there will be no one to disturb me. Since she would be at the college, I will have the whole house to myself during the day.

I drove straight to her house from the airport. Aayesha had told me where she kept the key of her apartment. I found it and entered the house. I had a quick bath made a cup of coffee for myself but I was too tired to drink it so I fell asleep and slept through the day. It was the clicking of the lock that woke me up. Aayesha had come and we met like long lost friend. Narrating the incidents, I told her that I needed change of job because I wanted to concentrate on writing books. I also told her about my meeting with Ashwin Solanki. Aayesha was serious when I told her how he had come into my room in Angola. She said, "Suku, beware, Solanki is a married man and he appears to be very much in love with his wife, two days back I saw them at a wedding in Delhi, both looked happy". I don't know why I felt a twinge of regret.

Later that night switching on a news channel I saw him, it was some function, and he was the chief guest. He looked handsome as ever, his hair graying at the temples; there was a serious look on his face. I switched off the T.V and tried to sleep.

After two days in Delhi, I took a flight to Mumbai and the work absorbed me, within three days my article about the horrific experience in

Angola were in the newspaper, I had written the detailed account of the blast. The injuries received by Vishwas, Satish and the death of Mariana and other journalists. I had given a detailed account of Mariana's death, her delivery, birth of Mark, his condition in the hospital, arrival of his father. Each word flew out of my pen as if I could not control it. At the end of it, the article became a moving tribute to all those who had lost their lives, their body parts and my dear Mariana.

I received innumerable letters and e-mails in appreciation of my article. On the second day of publication of the article I received a phone call on my office number, it was Ashwin Solanki "Your article has moved me Sukriti, but your bravado at Angola left me deeply disturbed" he said.

I remembered what Ayesha had said about seeing him at a wedding, looking 'happy'. I answered sarcastically "Mr Solanki, I am touched by your concern, I am too humble a person to deserve your concern. I am sure Mrs. Solanki will not appreciate this gesture".

There was silence on the other end and then the phone was disconnected.

"Serves him right ", I said to myself but I was feeling uneasy. May be he had meant it out of goodness of his heart. However, 'what about his passionate behavior in the hotel room in Angola!' I was confused.

My article had caught the fancy of Mr Surinder Katoch, the famous cine director, who was much acclaimed for directing meaningful films. His films had won accolades at the international festivals. He visited me in the office one day with the offer to buy the rights of my article. Mr Katoch wanted to make a film on this and had already roped in a well-known screenplay writer. I was thrilled at the offer but I had some reservations that at no cost would true events be undermined or exaggerated. I did not want any injustice done to the dead people. He agreed and we appointed to meet on the following Sunday and sign the contract.

There was much jubilation in the office and we all ended up in a bar, drinking and celebrating. Next day Mr Katoch's press statement was released about this offer. My family was ecstatic for me. I did not have much time to gloat over my success because I had to cover the by-election to Parliament from the reserved constituency in North-East. This seat had fallen vacant due to the sitting MP losing his seat under Anti-defection Act. It was a prestige election for the ruling party; Prajya Party and the People's Party. Stalwart politicians of both the parties were campaigning vigorously, addressing the public meetings, holding rallies. Ashwin

Solanki was also coming to address one rally. I had come to know about it the previous day when media was being briefed about the campaigning schedule. I thought it would be good to see Ashwin Solanki in his favorite territory.

Next day dressed in my customary jeans and a loose shirt; I set out for the venue of the meeting. Ashwin was to accompany the president of Prajya Party, his maternal uncle. Their helicopter landed one hour behind schedule and they drove straight away to the venue. The members of the media were sitting in an enclosure on the right side of the dais. I was in the third row, I could see Ashwin wearing a black safari suit and looking extremely relaxed while the party president was addressing the mammoth crowd. I saw Ashwin glance towards the press enclosure and he saw me. I quickly averted my glance. He addressed the gathering for a few minutes; the usual stuff that politicians speak at such times. It was the month of August and the weather was sultry. It was unbearable so I left the venue before his speech could end, as I wanted to interact with the people in the streets to gauge the mood of the electorate. There seemed to be lot of resentment among the people against the ruling party, for not doing much for the state. I spent four hours talking to the shopkeepers, Students, office goers, homemakers even the auto drivers to see what they felt about their candidates.

When I returned to my hotel room, I was exhausted and felt grimy all over my body. After a quick shower I ordered a light meal and was about to get into bed when my cell phone rang. It was Ashwin Solanki on the other end "Hello Sukriti, nice to see you after a long time" he said.

"Hello Sir, yes it is indeed nice. I hope the campaigning is going well" I said, for I was surprised that he should want to talk to me after my rudeness. He gave me no inkling that he was angry with me but went on taking about the general mood of the electorate and also how his party candidate was not making much head way with the people. He told me that his remarks were off the record and not to be quoted. I listened gave my comments and he hung up.

In spite of my tiredness, sleep was far from my eyes. Whenever I spoke to him I felt a deep stirring within me. Was I getting attracted to him! No, I said vehemently. I had been in love before. I was not like babe in the wood. This was just a passing cloud. I said to myself.

Back in Mumbai, two days later I was getting ready to meet some friends in a restaurant. My phone rang; Ashwin Solanki was on the line "Are you at home?" 'Yes I said. "I am coming' he said "But why. I . . .

mean . . . When . . . . Sorry." I was totally confused, why should he want to come and how does he know about my house! I could not think straight.

"I am already outside your door". I heard Ashwin's voice. Holding the cell phone in my hand, I ran towards the door and sure enough, he was standing there. Wearing a black suit he looked as if he was coming from some function. "May I come in". He smiled and I let him in.

"Always barging on you Sukriti; you must hate my manners". I made no comment. He walked up to the couch, dropped himself into it, rested his head against the cushions, and put his hand on his forehead.

"You look tired, I will get some coffee for you" I felt nervous in his presence I needed to regain my composure.

He said nothing so I went into my little kitchen to make some coffee for him. My mind was busy thinking why he had taken the risk of coming to my house. When I returned with the coffee mug; I found him sprawled full length on the couch and sleeping. I did not have the heart to wake him up. I gently pushed in the cushion under his head, covered him with a sheet, turned off the bright light, and put the night bulb on. I called up my friends making excuse that one of my relations had arrived from Delhi and I could not come. I sat on the sofa chair and watched him sleeping peacefully. I was perplexed that a public figure so well guarded by commandos should slip away, to come to my house. Where are his guards! What excuses he may have given! Why has he come! Surely, he could have slept at home, I drifted into sleep. Suddenly I felt a warm hand on my head, with a start I opened my eyes and saw Ashwin standing.

"Get up Sukriti, sleep in your bed' I was now fully awake.

"No, I am ok, I had made some coffee but you had fallen asleep" I said.

"You know what, I am indeed hungry. Can I invade your refrigerator"? Ashwin said.

"I will make you an omelet and some sandwich. Have you had your dinner"?

"No, I arrived in Mumbai in the evening to attend my cousin sister's wedding. I Stayed for half-an hour at the wedding and quietly left the venue to come here".

"How did you know where I lived? I asked.

"Madam I have my means". He said and teasingly pulled my nose and we burst out laughing.

I went into the kitchen, he followed me there, and I broke the eggs while he beat them with a fork. We looked a perfect picture of domestic harmony working in the kitchen, I smiled at my own foolish thoughts. I also made some cheese sandwiches and some coffee and carried them into my living room and ate our frugal meal in silence.

Suddenly he said 'Sukriti, you must be wandering why I behave like this, why I surprise you by my sudden appearance. I am attracted to you. I cannot get you out of mind.

"But . . ." I protested.

He did not let me complete the sentence. "I know I am a married man, holding a responsible position. I should not behave like a sixteen year old boy. However, Sukriti God knows how hard I have tried to forget you; I often tell myself that you are a young girl; you have a great future ahead of you. I am forty-five years old. My attraction to you can be fatal for my career and my marriage but I do not seem to care. I just want to hear your voice, see you, and hold you in my arms".

I was blushing while I could hear my violent heart-beats. His words were doing strange things to my heart, stirring passion, which I had long suppressed.

"Say something, Sukriti say, you are not angry with me, you don't dislike me". He pleaded sitting down on the carpet near my chair.

"No, I am not angry, but scared for you. Your visit to my house can give a lot of fodder to your political detractors. You are jeopardizing your career for a momentary weakness. I am not worth all that you will be losing in the process. We are both adults, not looking for flings. I do not approve of clandestine relationship with a married man. I am a middle class girl with middle class values". I said in calm voice.

He held my hands and kissed them. "Sukriti I understand the repercussions of this relationship. There is a lot at stake, your reputation; you are a young single girl with dreams of marriage. But what can I do, I am hopelessly in love with you. While I am married to someone and attracted to another it is not easy for me also". His voice was sad. He looked so vulnerable sitting on the carpet. I pulled his head on my lap and stroked his head. We sat like that for a very long time and then he stood up pulled me to my feet and put some cushions on the carpet and pulled me down. We lay there in each other arms, like two lost soul, each immersed in his own thoughts. At some point in the night, we fell asleep.

I woke up and found my head resting on his arm while he lay stretched full length along my back. The warmth emanating from his masculine frame was seeping into the core of my being. I thought whatever future our relationship may have, I would cherish this moment to my dying day.

He stirred besides me, smiled lovingly, and held me tightly. He kissed me on my lips and then he got up with a start, "I have to catch the 6 a.m. flight. My staff car is at my aunt's house. My guards must be going crazy for me. Let me go". He went into the wash room while I handed him the towel and comb.

Later I took out my car from the basement parking and I went to drop him. He held my arm tightly as I drove him. I left him a few meters away from his aunt's house. As he was getting down from the car, a beautiful tall lady of my age in track suit suddenly appeared and hugged him. I was scared.

"Dada, where have you been? I have been looking all around for you, thinking you had checked into same hotel. I did not wish to disturb you so I did not call". She said breathlessly.

I looked the other way undecided whether I should drive away. Ashwin turned towards me and said "Meet my younger sister, Reena. She is a doctor and lives in Delhi. She has also come to attend the wedding. Reena this is Sukriti."

She was watching me intently. 'Hello Dr Reena' I said.

"You are the famous journalist and the writer Sukriti Kaul; I am glad to meet you". Reena said pleasantly and after exchanging few niceties, I drove away wondering how Ashwin was going to explain our being together at an unearthly hour.

Later Ashwin told me that Reena had covered up for him when his relatives had searched for him. After this I met Dr. Reena again at a function in Delhi and we started talking on phones, nothing personal but about careers and likings in general. I found that Reena was very close to her brother and was married to her childhood sweet heart Dr. Sadanand Kirki.

How much of our secret she had guessed, I had no idea but sometimes while calling me she would talk about Ashwin and the great work he was doing for the country and his party.

After that meeting at my house in Mumbai I did not meet Ashwin for a long time. He was travelling a lot but he would often SMS me from different cell numbers. Telling me in code words that he missed me. I had also started missing him. I would see him in my dreams; they were strange visions, too childish at my age to ever think about. I would often lie down on the spot on my carpet where I had lain with him, touching the spot with great tenderness as if I was touching Ashwin. What was happening to me! I was proud of my self-control. The last time I had broken up with my boy friend of five years, I had promised myself that love was not meant for me. I was happy to be single and wanted to stay this way. My father would often drop hints about this boy or that boy. My sister-in-law Ajay's wife often reminded me that when she was of my age she was the mother of two children. I had stopped visiting my family, their incessant talk about marriage bored me. Now I would find myself thinking of marriage. Could there ever be such an eventuality! No; not with the man I would like to.

I often wondered why Ashwin and his wife had no children. Was she so career minded that children did not form a part of her plan! My curiosity was satisfied by Reena, one day while talking about her eight year old son Vishu, she said that she and her husband liked to discipline him in—their own way but since he stayed so much with her mother he was getting pampered "I cannot blame mummy for indulging Vishu, poor ma has been longing for Dada's child since so many years". Reena had sighed.

"May be Mr. Solanki and his wife are not too keen on children". I tried to be sympathetic.

"I think Radhika Bhabhi has some problem, though she blames Dada for not being able to father a child. I had suggested to her to have proper medical treatment done. She says that her doctor has told her that there is nothing wrong with her". Reena confided in me "I am too embarrassed to suggest any treatment to Dada. My husband had once tried talking to him to have himself examined by a leading fertility doctor; Dada brushed the idea so vehemently that he had no heart to pursue the matter". Reena said regretfully.

So this is what the truth was. Were Ashwin and his wife compatible, did they love each other !were some questions which assailed me often. I would have liked to imagine that Ashwin was not in love with his wife, she was a difficult woman to live with, but these very often are not the reasons for husbands drifting away. They do so despite wives being loving, successful and beautiful. I often felt a sense of guilt about the whole things. What right did I have to covet other woman's husband!

In my practical state of mind, I would put the blame on Ashwin that it is his betrayal, he had made commitment to cherish and love his wife, I had made no such commitment. But the fact was I should have resisted and not fallen in love with him. Ashwin had warned me about his being married. If he was happily married man, why was he being drawn to me! I drove comfort from this thought that there was something wrong with his marriage and that is why he was attracted to me. Now looking back on those times I think heart has its own reasons that cannot be explained by any logic or rationality. You fall in love with the wrong person because you are destined to make this mistake and suffer the consequences.

CHAPTER 6

Surinder Katoch was making the film on my story and he invited me once on the sets to see the film being shot. He introduced me to the artists who were playing different roles. There was a French artist who was playing the part of Mariana. She was tall like her and by the marvel of the make-up she was made to resemble Mariana a great deal. I was happy that the screenplay writer had done full justice to the story and there was not much change from the original story.

I was in touch with Oliver. He also sent me Mark's photographs. I loved them. He was growing to be a healthy chubby baby and looked so much like Mariana.

There was nothing exciting going on in my life except of course my feelings for Ashwin, although I avoided any situation where I would be thrown into his proximity, about which he often complained "Sukriti, we must meet soon or I will go out of my mind". He would plead and suggest ways of meeting. I was very fearful for him. I had to make excuses about being busy, whether he saw through my lies, I don't know but he never complained.

Around this time, I volunteered to take up the assignment of the finance analyst for my newspaper and my colleague Mr. Sundram took up my position as a political analyst. So I was mostly relegated to my office and I was glad that I had no need to get into any kind of situation where Ashwin and I will be thrown together and in due course of time he will get over me. Though this thought made me sad, one had to understand the ground realities.

My elder brother Ajay had seen a match for me and he was insisting that I should at least meet him once. "Sukriti don't be stubborn, life can get very lonely." He said "give yourself a chance to meet someone, you may like him". How like Ajay, philosophical and persuasive in his ways. I promised him that I would come to Delhi in a few days time and meet this man.

A day before I was to leave for Delhi, I received a call from Ashwin "Sukriti I have taken four days off and I am going to Almora in Uttarakhand, my friend has a cottage there. Would you like to come . . . think over it? If your answer is no, I will understand" he said calmly "I am leaving for Delhi tomorrow. My brother has seen some boy for me, and he insists that I should at least meet him." I saw no reason to hide the truth of my visit to Delhi from him.

He was quiet for a long time and then said,'" Oh I see! But should you change your mind, I am sending you the address of the cottage". He disconnected.

I thought over the matter a great deal and decided that this relationship will only give me heartbreak and may even cause a scandal if it ever leaks out, I was not brave enough and I had to think of my family.

Next day as I had planned, I left for Delhi and was glad that I had come. My father had grown old and weak. He wanted to see me married. My second brother Ganesh and his wife had also come. My prospective bridegroom came to my brother's house. He was a NRI and worked in Seattle in USA as a chemical engineer. He was thirty-five years old and belonged to Brahamin family from North India. From all accounts, he was what my brother would like to call an "eligible groom; a good husband material" He had the pedigree and was reserved and we spoke a little about his job and my job. His parents came to visit us next day and informed my father that he had liked me. I saw no reason in withholding my consent after all I wanted respectability in a relationship and this was it. There was celebration all around and February 14, was considered auspicious for our birth signs for betrothal ceremony. I returned to Mumbai the third day assuring my to-be bridegroom that I would meet him before he left for USA. Ashwin had not called me in all these days.

On reaching my apartment I was suddenly seized by doubt. Why had I given my consent to marriage! I was making a mistake getting into a marriage with a total stranger while I was yearning for another man! Was I not cheating this unsuspecting man! These thoughts were haunting me even when I reached my office.

There was plenty of work demanding my attention and soon I was absorbed in work. Later that afternoon I received a call from Reena.

She had called me after a long time. She had been very busy getting her nursing home built and now she was planning to start it.

"Mummy had consulted the 'Pandits' for the auspicious day for inauguration of the hospital but Dada's illness has stalled it now". Reena said.

My heart missed a beat; Ashwin was ill what has happened, where is he now? Wasn't he in Almora?

Trying to keep my voice from shaking, I asked Reena, "What has happened to Mr Solanki? Where is he?"

"Dada had gone to Almora to spend a few days in his friend's cottage. On the very first night of his stay, he had a heart attack. He was all alone in the house but he managed to call his P.A. in Delhi who arranged for immediate medical aid in the local hospital. My husband brought him back to Delhi two days back in a chartered plane. Dada is now in AIIMS". Reena gave me all the details of his illness and also how he had been under lot of stress. I felt terribly sad and guilty. It is my fault. I should have gone to Almora.

"Bhabhi was in Sweden when this happened and has reached India yesterday." Reena said.

After saying some appropriate words of sympathy, I hung up. My mind was disturbed. I felt a terrible sense of sadness growing in my heart. I could only curse my stupidity how can I ever ask for his forgiveness! What if something had happened to him! He had chosen to go to Almora to be with me for few days. While I was planning my marriage, Ashwin had been on the throes of death. This thought made me uneasy and later at home, I cried inconsolably and promised myself that I will visit him. I called up Reena late at night. She could guess from my depressed tone that something was bothering me. I told her that since I knew her brother personally, I would like to visit him, if he was allowed visitors; Reena at once agreed and promised to be in the hospital when I came.

I took the morning flight from Mumbai and reached Delhi by 10' o clock. I had informed Ayesha that I would be in Delhi and told her the reason of my visit. She had the same advice for me 'keep away he is a married man', but realizing my sorrow; she sighed and assured me that she would be waiting for me at home since she was having mid-term break in the college. Ayesha took one look at my face and knew that she could not dissuade me from meeting Ashwin. I cried bitterly and told her everything, my meetings with Ashwin, his visit to my apartment, his confession of love. Ayesha heard patiently and said nothing but I could see she was not happy about this.

I called up Reena in the evening. I reached AIIMS along with Ayesha, it was visiting time. In the lounge outside the VIP ward I could see a long line of visitors sitting. Ashwin's wife was also sitting and talking to them. The moment she saw us she stood up and took us inside the room. My heart was beating violently. I saw Ahwin propped against the pillows looking pale his eyes closed, his wife gently touched him on the arm, he opened his eyes and saw us, I greeted him nervously and he nodded his head in acknowledgement with a dead pan expression. Reena went on talking about his health and discussing the details of the medicine. I stood quietly, my eyes fixed on the wall. At length he turned to me we exchanged formal sentences about his health. I was painfully conscious of his wife, who was standing near her husband and holding his hand possessively. At one point I fixedly looked at it while talking to Ashwin, he hastily pulled his hand away and tucked it under the sheet. After another few minutes Ayesha and I took my leave. On the way to Ayesha's apartment we were both silent. I was beginning to see the logic behind Ayesha's advice.

Ashwin stayed in the hospital for another week and whenever he was not attended by his wife, he called me and we spoke of his health, we were both steering clear of any personal issues. For a long time I could not erase from my mind the scene in the hospital. I could detect sadness in his tone whenever he spoke to me. I wanted him to be happy. I would try to regale him with some funny anecdotes of my journalistic career. Once he hinted that he was missing me, I changed the topic.

I had also made up my mind that I shall not go ahead with my engagement; in fact I called up Ajay and told him that I could not get myself to marry a stranger. My brother reasoned out with me that the man was a good person, he would keep me happy but I was adamant so in exasperation Ajay disconnected. Nobody from my family brought the talk of marriage again; maybe they had given up on me. This time was depressing time for me because my peace of mind was disturbed.

Reena called me every day; I think she may have detected her brother's interest in me. She was too good natured to find faults with others. One day she called me to say that she was in Mumbai to attend a medical seminar and was free in the evening if I had no engagement that evening we could meet. I picked Reena from the hotel and we went to

Leela Kempinski to have dinner. I saw that Reena was quiet throughout the drive. "You are very quiet. All is well?" I asked.

"Yes, Yes! I am fine," Reena said and lapsed in silence again.

Later when we were having wine I again prodded Reena about her silence.

"Sukriti, I am worried about Dada."

"What happened, is he not out of the hospital?" I asked, I had spoken to him that morning and I knew he was back home.

"No, it is not about his health, but about him."

"Do you wish to talk about it?" I asked, though I was nervous.

"Sukriti I don't know how to say it, but I have to be frank. Please forgive me if I upset you. You know my brother is in love with you." I must have made some sound of surprise, but Reena continued, "Are you not aware of this? He loves you to distraction. I think his heart attack was also caused by the stress he is under. I know he does not have much feeling for Bhabhi now, thought he is married to her. This is affecting his health otherwise at the age of forty five Dada should not have had this problem. I often find him ignoring Bhabhi, avoiding any intimacy with her."

I listened apparently calm but inside I was shaking with apprehension. Reena said, "I am not being judgmental about my brother's feelings for you but, but this will only bring him unhappiness." Then she asked me, "Sukriti are you also in love with my brother?"

I mustered enough courage to say, "Yes Reena, it is sad but true that I also love your brother, despite the hopelessness of our situation I cannot help my feelings."

Reena did not comment and after inquiring about her son and husband we finished the dinner in silence and I drove her to the hotel.

I tried calling Ashwin but there was no reply so I presumed that he might be sleeping or his wife might be around. I felt depressed and tried to divert my mind from Ashwin by reading a novel I had recently purchased. I was going over that evening's conversation with Reena and wandering what she must be thinking about us, Ashwin's SMS came "I am fit and fine and Sukriti I want to meet you. Tell me where." I replied that I was out of town.

One evening when I returned to my apartment I was dead beat and went to sleep immediately. Some noise wake me up, it was my cell phone ringing, Ashwin was on the line" I have to meet you, if you don't want to meet me, tell me so and I will never bother you again" he said.

"What do you want me to say; you are inviting trouble for yourself. Have you ever thought what this will do to your political career and marriage?" I was losing my patience.

"I love you and nothing else matters to me except being with you, I am ready to resign from my post as well as from my seat if you want, tell me Sukriti, what do you want I will do anything". He sounded desperate.

"Ashwin please, just think you are a married man, you have to think of your wife, your family. You cannot throw away everything for a woman and I am not so stupid that I will believe you that you will love me forever. Now please go to sleep, tomorrow you will be able to think clearly with fresh mind and perhaps laugh at the whole drama." I hung up. He called me many times but I did not answer the call.

However, I could not sleep.

Next day at the office I received a call, it was Reena. She sounded worried, "Dada is considering resigning from the council of ministers. He may meet Uncle today".

"Oh!" Was all I could speak? I felt trapped.

I called him on his private number, I promised to meet him if he would reconsider his decision. He assured me that he will not take any hasty step until we met. I told him that I was going to Chandigarh on some work, my friend had a beautiful cottage in Chahal in Himachal Pradesh, in the neighbouring state of Punjab, and we could meet there, if it was safe for him to come there. He sounded ecstatic.

We travelled separately. I came by hired car from Chandigarh which I drove myself and Ashwin came by a car from Delhi to Shimla and then reached Chahal by a taxi. We had planned to reach the cottage together so that the care taker does not find our coming separately odd. It was 6 p.m. when my car touched Sadhu Ghat. I found Ashwin waiting by the side of the road. He got into the car and we drove off. I felt like a teenager going on my first date. Ashwin looked thin and pale. He smiled at me and held my hand throughout the 10 km drive to our retreat.

It was a beautiful cottage situated on a hill top and surrounded by pine trees. The rooms had been done up in pastel colors of blue and green. As soon as the care taker left after serving us tea, Ashwin pulled me in his arms. There was no roughness, but extreme love and tenderness as he kissed my eyes, my forehead and my cheeks, I found my reserve melting away and I responded to his love.

Later that night when we lay together in bed, I felt as if it was the most natural thing to do . . . He possessed me with tenderness as if afraid that he might hurt me. Later on as we lay satiated, he said, "You have made me the happiest man of this world." I snuggled close to him and kissed him. At that moment I had no thought of what tomorrow may hold for me or that I was behaving in a scandalous way. We drifted into sleep, woke up, made love passionately and we slept again. Next day I woke up late and to my surprise found him looking bathed and fresh.

My heart filled with love for him. I used to often wonder what he had seen in me, I was good looking with a slender body and taller than the average girls; so was his wife. What had drawn him to me? I could not stop myself from asking him. He thought for a while and said, "At my age you don't fall in love with a person just because of beauty or intelligence but because that person satisfies some deep urge in you. I cannot pin point one fact and say I love you Sukriti because of this or that quality. Love is never calculated or manipulated. Ever since I met you at the press conference and you crossed swords with me, I liked your fierce attitude and conviction. That afternoon at your grandmother's house in Srinagar when you slipped and fainted you looked so helpless, I felt very protective towards you, after that day I began to think of you quite often. The day I heard about the bomb blast in Angola and that you were at that site, I was out of my mind with worry. It was then I realized that I was in love with you. Now don't ask me why I love you because I myself have not been able to fathom the reason."

This answer pleased me and I loved him even more. We spent the whole day talking, narrating incidents of our life, family, college life, our career. There was this perfect ease between us as if we had known each other for ages. Later that evening I took him to the antique temple of Kali situated eight kilometers from Junga on a hill. It was dusk when we reached there. Out of hesitation I stayed behind when he entered the temple but he pulled me along and we offered our prayers to the Goddess Kali together. We stood together and when I was kneeling in reverence before the deity suddenly he took my hand in his and said, "I love you; I may not be able to legalize our relationship as long I am in public life but you will always have sole right on my love".

I thought about his last words for a long time, surely he had physical obligations towards his wife. She had right on his body, but I did not ask him what his relationship with his wife was. This was a chapter I was never going to discuss with him. Perhaps he too had seen my perplexity as we were coming back from the temple he said, "Sukriti I meant every word I said in the temple. Ever since I have fallen in love with you, I have kept myself away from any physical contact with Radhika. I know I am not being fair to her but how can I touch her when it is you I am thinking about all the time."

I felt happy. Which woman would not feel happy to know that she has monopoly over the heart and body of the man she loves! One part of me was ready to disbelieve him; was he saying this to win my trust or get me into his bed! Now that he had succeeded in getting his way, what now! I would often wonder during those days but he had no reason to lie to me I had never chased him or wanted anything out of him. I never discussed our future or his marriage. I had convinced myself that, I had nothing to do with that side of his life. In fact I was not even thinking of the future. Just living life with him from one day to another

How those days flew, I have no idea. Every moment with him was so tender, so beautiful that I just wanted to store them in memory. I discovered many things about him, like sleeping on his back with one arm thrown across his eyes, getting up very early in the morning, and tending to plants, his love for Indian classical music. It was hard for me to believe that the hard-core bureaucrat turned politician had an aesthetic side to him. One morning, on waking up late as usual, I found him humming an old film song, his voice was good and he was perfectly in tune. I commented on his talent, "Ashwin I am discovering your hidden talents every day, I thought beyond public speaking and politics you were not interested in anything." He smiled that disarming smile of his, "Politics is a hard food, and one needs these digestives to digest it. Sometimes I think I should have pursued my singing professionally, but I had to follow family tradition of joining the civil services, my dad, my uncles all had dreams for me; Bhaskar uncle did not marry, he entered politics, being the only nephew I had to live his dreams also. So I am fulfilling the aspirations of other people, not my own. When I married Radhika I had hoped to have a peaceful life, one or two children, but . . . .".

He appeared so vulnerable at that moment that I had a strong urge to hug him and just hold him.

Later that evening he received a call from his Bhaskar Uncle, directing him to reach Delhi at once because some conflict had broken out in their party in a particular state over the nomination of the Chief Ministerial candidate. The state politicians wanted the CM to be from the state and not someone thrust from outside. Ashwin who was known to enjoy sufficient clout with some senior members of the state party was being sent for damage control. As soon as he received this call, he became serious and looked at me appealingly as if he was pleading with me to let him go. I assured him that I will drop him at Shimla from where a private helicopter was being sent to take him to the state capital that very night. I packed his things and made sure that he had not left anything behind. Before departure he held me tightly in his arms and kissed me passionately. "I am sorry Sukriti to spoil your holidays. You see this is the reason I want to get away from politics. I want a peaceful life with you. We could have stayed for few more days. Why don't you stay behind and enjoy your stay. Call your friend from Delhi. I will have her booked on the next flight from Delhi to Chandigarh. I will book a taxi for her to Chahal; it is just a three hours journey from there." It was so like him to plan everything so meticulously and expect people to fall in with his plans.

"Doesn't it occur to you that Ayesha is a working lady? She may have commitments. Now you go. I will stay behind and explore this place on my own. You don't have to worry". I said. He said nothing but from the way he looked at me I could guess that he was sorry.

We drove in silence till Shimla and I dropped him a few miles away from the helipad, not wishing to cause him embarrassment. On my way back my mind was filled with thoughts of Ashwin and I also thought of our relationship, where will it go from here. May be it, will be a long time till we meet again, in private, it may be weeks or months; who knows!

On my return to the cottage, I felt miserable and lonely. So next day I left Chahal and drove to Chandigarh where I returned the car and took the night flight to Mumbai. Ashwin had called me on reaching the state capital; he had been worried about me; apologetic that he had to leave me suddenly. I assured him that we had entered a relationship where we cannot expect much from each other and our meetings were subject to many constraints so we must get used to it. I was trying to be brave but I knew I wanted to cry and tell him that I was missing him.

Back in Mumbai I tried to get my life back to my normal routine. I could not concentrate on my work. My articles were becoming dull, uninspiring and there were one or two letters to the editor wondering why my pen had lost its old sharpness. I was particularly becoming partial in my praise for the ruling party and my colleagues noticed it. They would often tease me 'a hard core socialist is becoming republican.' Contact with Ashwin was confined to nightly calls from wherever he was at that time. He kept assuring me of his love, his promises to love me forever. I told him I believed him, but my mind was not assured. His popularity was rising. People were seeing him as a progressive leader who was honest and worked diligently. The media was making him out to be the Gen Next leader. It made me very happy and also put me on my guard that any wrong move from his side or my side would destroy everything for him.

One evening while watching late news, I saw Ashwin with his wife. He was being felicitated and his wife stood by his side beaming. At one point he smiled at her, there was something in that look that one can only interpret as love, tenderness, it disturbed me to no end, and I went into fits of depression. I was losing interest in my job. In fact, I was losing interest in everything around me. Later on I saw him many times at different events and his wife was always by his side. I kept thinking whether he was cheating both of us!

Around this time, the film based on my article was released. It was a beautifully made film and I was invited for its premier. The critics paid glowing tribute to its story and all congratulated me. There were many cine stars at the function, one famous star hugged me and those pictures were flashed in all the newspapers. Ashwin congratulated me on my success the next day but he seemed disturbed by the photograph, though he did not say much, he taunted me about having found many admirers in the film line.

Past few weeks had been depressing for me and to hear him talk like this, my pent up frustration came out, I said, "That should make you happy, you will have genuine reason to dump me and go on becoming a happily married man for shutter bugs." He heard silently and then hung up. This made me more angry. I called him but he did not answer my calls. I lay awake the whole night, thinking that my life cannot go on like this. For the first time in my life I was insecure. Ayesha had warned me of this. She had told me that I will always be the other woman; the guilty woman, whom people will see as a mistress or a time pass of the young politician. This is not what I had wanted. God knows how I had fought against it. I had resisted but fate had willed otherwise. Here I was, hopelessly in love with a famous man, who was married to a woman of substance. I felt cheap, terribly cheap for having slept with a married man. I had to get away from this situation; I had to take hold on myself. I cried myself to sleep and next morning I woke up with a new determination.

I called up Ayesha and told her everything about my trip to Chahal and my life afterwards. She heard me silently and then suggested that I should change my job. I should take to writing books, since I was good at it. This will give me the freedom to move wherever I wanted and there was good money also in it. "Get out of your safe cocoon and explore life. There is more to your life than Mr. Ashwin Solanki, you will have the world at your feet", Ayesha narrated horrifying story of a certain politician who had recently had his mistress killed when he feared that, she was pregnant. "These people have no scruples", Ayesha was cynical about these relationships, having suffered heartbreak once she was quite wary of getting into it again. Her suggestion appealed to me. I Knew I could do this.

Chapter 7

Few years back I had collected some material about the customs of a particular tribe in Jaunsar Hills of Chakrata in Uttrakhand where in some areas polyandry was still prevailing. Some sociologists had traced this custom to the Mahabharata time when Draupadi had married five Pandvas. The more I thought of it the greater my enthusiasm became that I would base my story on this theme. I had to have authentic knowledge of those customs to be able to do justice to my story. I will have to spend considerable time in Chakrata, meet the people, consult the archives, and talk to local historians to make my story authentic. One week later I put in my resignation papers.

The editor-in-chief Mr. Mallingam was sad to let me go. "I will miss you," he said as he hugged me. I had told him about my desire to become a full time writer. He told me that I could pursue my writing along with my journalistic career, "How will you support yourself while writing, you know books take months even years to complete," the fatherly Mr. Mallingam said to me. On the day of the farewell he quietly put in my hand a folded paper it turned out to be a cheque of five lakh rupees. He said that it was his parting gift. My voice was choked with emotions. I hugged him and all my colleagues. Partings with loved ones can be so painful! At that time there seemed lot of sadness in my life.

All this while Ashwin had not called me, nor had I tried calling him. Though occasionally, I did see his images on the television attending meetings or inaugurating something. I was determined not to allow myself to weaken. The first thing I had to do was to acquire a new cell number and leave Mumbai.

I had some friends from college settled in DehraDun and when I called them and told them about my plans they were happy to help me. Ashraf Ahmad was my classmate in Post graduate class. He had been courting a Hindu girl, Gayatri a year junior than us in college. I was the mediator, the postman as well as the arbitrator whenever they had a fight. During our internship with a leading Delhi English Newspaper, Ashraf and his Hindu girlfriend had a runaway marriage and I was the planner of this inter religion union. How frightened we were after the marriage! Expecting terrible communal backlash I had sent Ashraf and Gayatri to live with my elder sister, Suhasni in Kodaicanal. My sister who was an incurable romantic had welcomed them with open arms. Gayatri had left a letter for her parents informing them of her marriage; she had added that if they try to create problems for her or her husband, she would commit suicide. This last bit quietened her furious parents and they severed their relations with her. But before her father's death, love for his only daughter so overpowered the dying man that he left her all his property, which was quite substantial. Gayatri and Ashraf had purchased some land and orchards in Dehradun and were settled there. He was a freelance journalist and his articles were published weekly in the centre page of two premier New Delhi English Dailies. By all accounts their marriage could be called a successful one. They had one daughter who was around ten years old and was studying in the local public school.

I received a warm and loving welcome from both my friends and their beautiful daughter Gazalla, in DehraDun. I was happy to see that they were giving their daughter a secular upbringing and didn't impose their religion on each other. Their house was situated on the Mussoorie-Dehradun Road. One could see the Shivalik Range towering over the entire landmass. I have always had fascination for hills, having spent many years in Kashmir, living with Nanu. Ashraf accompanied me to Chakrata, situated 55 miles from Dehradun, it is a hilly journey. He introduced me to a local politician who had been a history teacher in the local government school, before he joined politics. I stayed in his house for many weeks, meeting people, visiting the local shops, talking to elderly people. When they came to know that I was writing a novel based on their culture they were happy but warned me to handle this issue with all delicacy of feelings. "This is our ancient revered culture, give it the due respect," one elderly native warned me. Slowly and gradually my story was shaping up, characters were emerging in my mind, there were so many legends I heard during my stay there that I was sure I would be able to get my events and my incidents. My heroine Kanwari and my hero Lakha Singh were born out of these stories.

After meeting the people during the day I would return to my host's house and straightaway head for my room and jot down all the new things I had heard. My heroine was a Jaunsari girl, the only daughter of a rich apple cultivator. She was married to the eldest son of a landlord and as per the custom of the land she was to be the wife of the other two brothers also. Being educated she opposed this tradition because she loved her husband Lakha Singh. My story revolved around her trials, her fight, and her acquiescence ultimately to this custom. The story was written from the point of view of Kanwari as well as from the perspective of Lakha Singh, his anguish, his jealousy to share his wife with his younger brothers and finally his defeat and escape from the village. I was so much fascinated by my characters that I fell in love with them, their sorrows became my sorrows and their struggle was like my struggle.

My writing kept me so engrossed that I had almost got over my personal frustration. I was enjoying each moment of my experience as a writer and wondered why I hadn't thought of it before. Ashraf, Gayatri and Gazalla came to take me back after nearly one and a half months. I did not realize so much time had gone by. I had completed two hundred pages of my novel and my plan was to add another hundred pages to it.

When I returned to Dehradun, it was monsoon season and the rains here can be torrential sometimes even beating the record of Cherapunji of Assam for recording highest rainfall in the world. Everywhere there were lush green plants, tress and mist rising from the Shivalik hills presented a picturesque scene. I would sit for hours in the veranda watching the rain and the foggy mountains. Ashraf and Gayatri used to entertain me with their romantic anecdotes, when they were courting each other, their stay with my sister at Kodaicanal and how they feared my disciplinarian sister. We would laugh and enjoy such tales. It was during one such session that Gayatri asked me why I had not married. "Surely there cannot be dearth of men for you; you are beautiful and famous," she said. Ashraf decided that he was going to become a match maker and keep his eyes open for some eligible bachelor. "Sukriti you are going to be thirty four years old, your biological clock is ticking. Marry now before it's too late. Do you remember the Tee Shirt one of our classmates used to wear which had 'Virginity causes cancer' printed on it and how our classmates would periodically offer themselves to prevent this dreaded disease from infecting her?" The memory brought great laughter and we remembered lot many things. Gayatri laughing her guts out said, "Ashraf you cannot imagine young liberated girls now being strangers to sex. World has changed so much."

Ashraf said, "No I don't believe you, look at our Sukriti darling, chaste and untouched. I am sure she will die a virgin." I smiled indulgently wondering what if I was to tell him about my amorous nights in Chahal with the famous Mr. Solanki. I am sure Ashraf would have looked at me in mock horror and said "et tu Brut".

I stayed five months in Dehradun and by this time autumn was setting in and my novel had nearly completed. The day I completed the last page, I felt a sense of loss as if I was separated from my dear friends. I suppose all writers feel this sense of loss.

Ayesha had arranged a meeting with the famous publisher in Daryaganj in Delhi. They had asked me for the manuscript of my novel in soft copy. Within a fortnight I received an email from them that they liked my story and would like to finalize the publishing details the remuneration and the royalty matters. I was excited, the new phase of my life was about to begin.

I reached Delhi in the month of October. The weather was pleasant and Ayesha was as usual happy to see me happier that I had forgotten Ashwin Solanki. The whole day I was busy, meeting the publisher, signing contract and to my great surprise the publisher was ready to buy my book at a whopping price of one crore. He had read my articles and knew the popularity I had achieved as a journalist. My book was a good business proposition for the publishing company.

"He is a businessman, he knows how he will earn from this book," Ayesha told me. Ayesha and I talked late at night about the book, her life, my life and of course Ashraf and his family. During the conversation Ayesha told me that she had met Dr. Reena a number of times at different social gatherings and she had been particularly asking for me. "She said she had tried your number several times but the number was out of service," Ayesha said. "I told her that you were living with your sister in Kodaicanal and writing some book," Ayesha continued. I wasn't keen to talk about Reena or her family. I had left that phase of my life in Mumbai.

Another week passed and I was busy selecting the cover of my book and having it printed. The publishers wanted a formal book release and they wanted some celebrity to release the book. I was not sure if I wanted to meet any celebrity at this point of time. They assured me that it would be someone from the literary field so I agreed. The date was fixed to be the 20 October and the book release ceremony was to take place in Hyatt Regency in South Delhi. The invitation cards were printed and to my horror it had the name of the Hon'ble Minister Mr. Ashwin Solanki who had consented to be the chief guest. I was angry, I refused to go. I told the publisher that I would not attend the function. The proprietor of the publishing company Mr. Hanif Ahmad could not understand my anger. Ayesha had to coax me into going. "If you have got over him, then why do you bother"? I was sad, very sad, why must fate bring me again face to face with Ashwin. God only knew with what difficulty I had pushed his thoughts out of my mind, and now to see him!

I wore a light colored chiffon saree with no makeup and tied my long hair into a loose bun. Ayesha was with me. I had invited my father and elder brother's family also because they were all in Delhi. I met my father and brother and his wife at the entrance of the hall. My father became very emotional and hugged me. He had gone very frail. My sister-in-law was still angry with me for having turned down the marriage offer. My brother Ajay was as usual chirpy and happy for me. We met like long lost friends and inquired about my other brother and sisters. Suddenly there was the announcement that the chief guest had arrived. My heart was beating so fast that I could hear it in my ears. Ayesha held my hand tightly. I did not go to receive him, Mr Ahmad and his subordinates went to receive him. There were a number of media personalities whom I personally knew. Ashwin was introduced to me by Mr Ahmad. I could see the dead pan expression with which he greeted me. I also exchanged greetings and sat down with my family. My family was introduced to Ashwin. I was surprised that he touched my father's feet respectfully and shook hands with my brother very warmly. He even exchanged warm words with my sister-in-law. A politician has to be charming in public, I thought sardonically. The function was presided over by my friend from the electronic media Gurinder Singh, who owned a very popular news channel. Mr. Ahmad talked about my previous work, my journalistic career and my latest book, and was happy to be associated with me and wished a long and fruitful association.

I was called to say a few words. I said that I would not wish to usurp the speaking prowess of the politicians. I did not have the art to win the hearts of the people with my impressive words all I wished to say is that this book is my sincere effort to bring to fore the lives of the people in the obscure hilly terrains of Himalayas and see how they have preserved their culture. I talked passionately about the economic hardships of these people, their daily struggle for survival against the hostile condition, their simplicity and love. "I have learnt from them the true meaning of love". When I stopped I heard a loud applause and saw Ashwin looking at me

In his address Ashwin praised my writing and called himself a great admirer of my political analysis and writing style. He felt that my leaving journalism was a great loss to the media but he was glad that I had taken to writing. Ashwin also mentioned my earlier article which had been made into a successful film. He called me a role model for the younger generation and wished me luck. He promised to read my book.

Gurinder Singh, known for his keen sense of humour commented that God was very partial to me, he had given me the beauty of body and brains and I was getting better and better with age like an old wine. He added in lighter vein that at one point of time he was my greatest admirer both professionally and romantically but I never noticed him which is his regret. This aroused a lot of laughter and I turned red in the face, as I looked up I saw Ashwin looking at me with a fixed stare.

The book was released amidst cheering and Ashwin approached me while I was talking to my friends from media. He said that I should sign a copy of the book that was gifted to him. I wrote 'The Hon'ble Minister Shree Ashwin Solanki, I hope you will find time to read this book, and appreciate the simple faith of the hill people un touched by deceit"

Throughout the event Ashwin was giving me furtive glances; I ignored this and went on laughing and chatting away. Soon he left as he had to attend another function. After the event my father and brother insisted that I should come to their house and spend the night with them. So I took Ayesha's leave promising to come to her house next evening.

At my brother's house my nephew and niece were eagerly waiting for me. I hugged them and we all sat down to catch up on all the things we had missed since my last meeting. My brother was very loving and had all my favorite dishes made by his cook and my sister-in-law served me with her own hands. Nobody discussed marriage, though my father did ask me about my future course of action. This made me think seriously about my present situation. It was a fact that I had nowhere to go; I had already vacated my Mumbai flat and cancelled the lease. I had spent five months like a nomad in Uttrakhand. Where was to I live! Where should I settle down!

With these thoughts in my head I went to sleep. Suddenly the cell phone woke me up. It was Ayesha, "Sukriti, Ashwin has come to my house. He wants to meet you. Please talk to him," she said. I was surprised he was the last person I would expect to visit me, but then Ashwin had always been like this. Hadn't he always barged in to my life?

I said, "Yes Mr. Solanki, tell me what is the matter?" I tried keeping my voice as emotionless as I could.

"You are a fine one to ask me what the matter is. You disappear all of a sudden and don't leave a trace of yourself. What was I to think? I don't think my feelings count for you. You are self-centered, selfish woman. You only consider your feelings and never realize how you must be hurting others," he said menacingly.

"Can we have this discussion later because my brother's room is next to mine and I cannot speak loudly," I said and hung up. The phone rang again. It was Ayesha, "Sukriti, Ashwin says he is coming to your brother's house to talk to you. I cannot stop him. Please talk to him yourself."

So I spoke to Ashwin again. This time politely explaining to him why I cannot meet him, he was adamant, "Either you meet me or I am coming over to your brother's house". Just to dissuade him I promised to meet him tomorrow in the evening at Ayesha's house. He was pacified and I disconnected. After that I could not sleep. I felt my life was falling into shambles again. This is not what I wanted, I was happy the way my life was going on. Next day the phone rang, it was Aahwin "Are you coming over?" I hastily took leave of my father and brother and left for Ayesha's house.

Ayesha was not at home when I reached. I always had duplicate key to her house. I went into the kitchen and cooked dinner for both of us I started tidying her room. Ayesha was working on her research paper; she spent most of her time in the library. Her house needed cleaning, so I tied an apron and spent the next four hours cleaning and re-arranging her house. After that I had a quick bath and sat before the television waiting for her arrival. It was around 7:00 p.m. when the doorbell rang. I rushed to open the door and to my utter dismay Ashwin stood there. My legs began to shake, had he not collected me in the arms I would have fallen. He picked me up as if I was a small child and held me to his heart. He was shaking with emotions and I could feel his heartbeat. He stood holding me like that for a long time and then with a deep sigh put me on my feet. I staggered and he steadied me and pulled me down on the chair while he stood towering over me. His voice was harsh, "Why did you go away like this? Tell me Sukriti, did you not trust me? I have promised my undying love and loyalty to you. That night you hurt me very deeply when you said that I would dump you and go back to being a happily married man; why did you say that?" he asked me.

"It doesn't matter now, Ashwin. We are two adults and must understand our compulsions. It was very silly of me to say those words. Forgive me, after that I tried calling you but you did not answer my calls So I thought you did not wish to talk to me," I answered calmly.

"I was hurt and you know my position, I have to keep up my public appearances as a family man. How could you could even think that I could dump you! Have you forgotten the temple; the promise I made? Sukriti why did you go away without telling me? You even changed your cell number. I have been in hell all these days. I sent Reena to meet Ayesha but Ayesha did not tell her your whereabouts. I even went to Chahal hoping to see you in the cottage. You left your job also. Why, why did you do this to me? Oh, Sukriti!" He held my shoulders in his menacing grip "Why did you have to leave me like that".

I could see his face, the grey hair around his temples and his face had gone thinner. There was a sad expression in his eyes. The frost in my heart began to thaw. He had suffered. I pulled him down on the chair next to me and held his hand. "Ashwin, after I returned from Chahal, I was miserable, loving you but being so far away from you. I could not concentrate on my work and then one day I saw you on the TV with your wife; you both looked so happy that the futility of my own situation hit me hard. I began to think that I was just an amusement for you. Your life lay with your wife. I decided to leave Mumbai and go somewhere, far away from you. I also changed my number so that nobody could call me. Only my family and Ayesha knew where I was. I thought if I did not see you and hear your voice, I will get you out of my mind and I had nearly succeeded when you came back. Why cannot you see that our love is doomed? This relationship has caused me immense pain. I have been haunted by guilt that I am a home breaker and I have no moral right to take you away from your wife "I began to weep as I said these words, the truth was, seeing him again my reserve was slipping away and I knew there would be nothing but pain and heartbreak for me.

Ashwin took me in his arms and let me cry. He kissed me gently on my lips and then with growing passion, I could feel his body becoming tense against mine and before I knew what was happening we were making love. Months of pent up emotion had come out like a deluge. I felt myself responding to his love making with equal passion. There was no holds barred. In the coupling of our bodies, I found our souls also getting united. I looked into his eyes and saw extreme love and tenderness. How could I have lived so far away from him! How could I ever imagine that he was playing deception on me! His may be legally bound to another woman but he loved me. For the first time since meeting him I felt that I could trust him, I could love him. No words were spoken, yet our silence was as eloquent as we explored each other with lips and hands and finally lay spent in each other's arms. I silently prayed to god, let me love him forever.

Ashwin thought that something was worrying me, "Sukriti, don't worry about the consequences of our love making. There will be no consequences. You know what I mean. As Radhika has so often told me that it was my fault that we did not have any child. So I suppose you need not worry about any consequences."

"No, this is not worrying me. Even if there were consequences, I will go ahead with it. A life conceived in love would be very precious to me because it will be a part of you and a part of me. But suppose this eventuality does arise what will be your decision?" I asked him hypothetically.

Ashwin laughed laudly, "My darling, this will not happen, you know Radhika's doctor has told me about my inability to father a child, and even if it happens I will be very happy to have a child with you. I will give up everything to own my child and you as its mother." There was a determination in his voice and it pleased me to hear his words. We talked for a long time and Ayesha arrived. She was not surprised to see Ashwin; somehow I guessed that she had deliberately stayed out late. We had dinner together, talked about the response my book had generated. critics had given my book good reviews and Ayesha's literary friends had found the book interesting. I was happy. Ayesha asked Ashwin to stay the night over if he could possibly. He agreed but made some phone calls and later he told me that he had called up Reena's husband to tell him to pick him up early in the morning. So Reena's husband knew and he had dropped Ashwin at Ayesha's house, earlier in the evening.

Ayesha gave us her bedroom because it had a double bed and she went to sleep in the guest room, which had a nice comfortable bed. We did not sleep the whole night but in between talking and making love we did not know how the time passed.

Before leaving the early morning next day, Ashwin insisted that I should stay in Delhi. He assured me that he will get his secretary to locate a nice apartment and he will buy it for me. "At least you will be closer to me, if you are in Delhi," he told me as he kissed me goodbye before leaving. He quietly walked out of the door and from my window I could see him get into a big black car and drive away. I went to bed and slept the whole day. Ayesha had a holiday so she also slept till late. Ashwin came to Ayesha's house quite often after that night and when he could, he stayed the nights stayed over and after spending our pent up passion, we lay peacefully in each other's arms talking late into the night. We did not discuss his work or his marriage but just ourselves.

Next two months occupied me completely. My book had been well received in the literary circles and sold record number of copies in one month. There were invitations pouring in, press wanted to interview me. One particular magazine wanted to do a feature on me, they felt my looks, and my being a spinster a famous journalist and a writer will appeal to the readers. I was a celebrity. My friend Surinder Katoch had read this book also and he was requesting me to sell the rights of the book to him, so that he can have a screenplay written. He was offering me a substantial amount; I agreed to meet him in Mumbai. Ashwin came to Ayesha's house that evening and, I told him about the offer and my intended visit to Mumbai. He was quiet, I could sense he did not want me to go but said, "If it will make you happy, go by all means, but you must come back to Delhi, I have already had some apartments shortlisted for you when you come back you can see them and then we will buy one. Promise me my darling that you will come back to Delhi." Ashwin was very insecure as far as I was concerned, he needed constant assurance that I loved him and I was not going to go away again.

My meeting with Surinder Katoch, his screenplay writer and various formalities in connection with signing of contract took almost a week. I also visited my old office and my former boss, Mr. Mallingam, he was overjoyed to see me and when I was leaving he said softly that he had an opening for me in his the Newspaper at Mumbai and he would be very happy if I would accept it. He assured me that it would not come in the way of my writing. I would have fixed office hours and weekends off.

The offer was tempting but I had to speak to Ashwin before taking any decision. When I reached the hotel I called up Ashwin, his number was busy. I tried another number but the call was diverted to the first number. So I could not speak to him until very late at night. He called me. He sounded tired, he said that Radhika was transferred back to India from Sweden and had been promoted to the rank of senior secretary in the Ministry of External Affairs. She was arriving two days later but she wanted Ashwin to come to Sweden to help her wind up her house there. He had tried to make excuses of 'prior engagements' but she got her way by weeping. So he was already in Sweden and helping her. "Sukroti I will be back in three days time, you must return soon to Delhi. I love you" I heard this in silence and after exchanging a few words we disconnected. I was on the verge of telling him about Mr. Mallingam's job offer but did not say anything. This was not the appropriate time. I kept awake for a long time, thinking about the changed circumstances at Delhi and the job offer. The prospect of settling in Delhi was no longer appealing to me. It would only cause me unhappiness and with Radhika firmly back in Ashwin's life, my living in Delhi made no sense. At least if I live in Mumbai I will have less opportunity of meeting Ashwin and then time is the best healer, I comforted myself.

Next day I went to visit some old friends in Colaba and spent the better part of the day with them. I did not want to give myself any time to think about Ashwin but stray thoughts did trouble me and occasionally I felt myself imagining him with his wife, sharing intimate moments, after all she was his wife. I spoke to Ayesha later that night about the job offer and return of Radhika; she was quiet for some time and then told me to 'give the offer a thought'. In the evening I called Mr. Mallingam and told him that I was ready to accept his offer. He was happy and called me the next day to join my duty.

CHAPTER 8

M y life had taken another turn. Sometimes winds prove too strong for wings and one has to let go of oneself with it. I called up Ayesha and told her about my decision. She said she would miss me but 'if this will make you happy, then I am happy for you.' I did not call Ashwin; I had nothing to tell him Next day I was back in the office and this time as an Editor and the boss. My old colleagues welcomed me with open arms and made sure that I was comfortable. I guessed that I needed to keep myself occupied.

I put my heart and soul in the newspaper and I had also started researching for my second novel and spent all my free hours before the computer downloading information about the background of my second novel. Ashwin was back in Delhi and perhaps helping his wife to settle down. He called me the moment he was in India and alone. He wanted to know why I hadn't returned to Delhi. I told him about the job and told him my intention to make Mumbai my base again. He pleaded with me to return, promising that he will find some way to meet. "I have also selected an apartment for you. Come back Sukriti, this time if you go away I will die" he said. I felt bad for him, for myself as well for the hopeless situation we had put ourselves in. I explained to him that it was the best way for us. "Let's see how it works, but I love you, remember this" I said to him to cheer him up.

After a few weeks the pain of separation began to hurt less. My career as an Editor was yielding positive result. Mr. Mallingam was gradually delegating lots of powers to me and I was working hard to justify his trust in me. My previous novel was still being talked about and my fans were eagerly awaiting the release of my second book. In social circles of

Mumbai I was a regular sight and the media was lapping up all that I said. There were young scribes hanging around to take my interview and I was beginning to enjoy this adulation.

Then the miracle happened! If I may call it a miracle. It was the third month of my return from Delhi, while coming to my office on the tenth floor, by the elevator I felt dizzy and then the spell went away. I reached the office and got busy in work. In the afternoon while going to the washroom, I felt the ground shifting under my feet and before I could steady myself, I fell on the floor. Thank god there was nobody in my office. I quickly got to my feet and called my personal assistant on the intercom to send me some coffee. I felt much better afterwards and the day passed on without any further incident. Next day while brushing my teeth I felt nausea rising in my throat and it happened many times during the morning. I must see the doctor; I told myself and made an appointment with a doctor whose number I could find on the telephone directory.

That evening after the office I went to the clinic and the doctor was a pleasant middle aged lady. She subjected me to thorough investigation asking me about my last periods. I often had irregular menstrual cycle so I told her that it was nearly the third month since I had had my periods. She asked me to give my urine for pathological test and I saw her take a little plaster chip and put a few drops of my urine in it. After observing the reaction, she dropped the bomb shell that I was ten weeks pregnant, which meant that I was in the third month of my pregnancy. I looked at her in disbelief. It was rather a shock, how could this have happened! Reena had told me about Ashwin's inability to father a child; Ashwin himself had told me that Radhika's doctor had told him that his sperm count was too low to impregnate a woman. Then how . . . when! No, surely there has been a mistake, I told the doctor. She assured me about the veracity of the test. She said this was a fool proof method of detecting pregnancy and there was no doubt in her mind that I was pregnant. She told me to touch my belly and feel the tightening of the muscle, a little bulge. I could feel it.

My first thought was of fear. The scandal it will cause, humiliation for my family, my father's and brothers" reaction. These thoughts assailed me as I sat in the car returning to my apartment. The driver dropped me at the gate of the building and my feet felt heavy as lead as I took the elevator to my apartment.

I had to think clearly, reasonably how I had to deal with this situation. I was visualizing Ashwin's reaction when I tell him this news. Will he believe me that the baby is his, because he sounded very convinced that he was incapable of fathering a child. What if he casts aspersion on my character, just to extricate himself from the situation! After all he had to think of his marriage, his career, his public image. I remembered the story Ayesha told me about a certain politician having his mistress killed when she got pregnant. I decided to wait for a few days before breaking this news to him. Unconsciously I was sparing myself the disappointment if he reacted sharply or denied the child to be his. The doctor had prescribed some medicine to stop morning sickness. I promptly started taking the medicine.

Never at any point of time did the thought of terminating the pregnancy occur to me. No doubt I was frightened but I could not think of getting rid of my baby. My religious beliefs did not permit me to think about it. Old fashioned it may sound to some but in my view it was a sin. I had to deal with it. I underwent another test in a bigger clinic, the result was the same. After a week's dilemma I disclosed the news to Ayesha. Her reaction was dismay but she soon recovered and offered to come to Mumbai for a few days and "together we would think what is to be done". I agreed and she was to come as soon as she got leave from the college.

Ashwin was calling me every night and at such times I pretended to be normal and even joked about our long distance love affair. In the office I kept myself busy and started wearing saris instead of trousers, my colleagues liked the change and Mr. Mallingam even commented that I was looking healthier. "Mumbai is suiting your health," he commented. I smiled.

When Ayesha arrived I was already in the twelfth week of pregnancy. Ayesha was unconventional in many matters. She asked me if I wanted to keep the pregnancy. I said, "Yes, it is my baby and I would like to bring it in this world."

"Would you like Ashwin to know about it?" Ayesha asked. I told her about Ashwin's belief, Radhika's doctor's statement. "Ashwin may not believe that it is his, you know I had gone out of his life for so many months." Ayesha agreed with me but comforted me that she would find some way out. During her one week stay with me, we only discussed my pregnancy, its repercussions on my career, my family and the child's own future. "Remember, we Indians are still conservative about having children out of wedlock. You really will have to be brave and face it all," Ayesha warned me. This frightened me even more.

Since the day I had been to the clinic, I had not slept well. I would wake up in the middle of the night shivering and my throat parched. My eyes were developing dark circles and I felt tired all the time. Ayesha had to return but before leaving she promised me that she will think of some way.

True to her words Ayesha had found a way, rather a surprising one! Four days after her departure, I was sitting at my desk at home giving last touches to the editor's page when the doorbell rang. Who could it be at this hour? I put on the safety chain on the door to peep out. I saw Dr. Reena standing outside. I was surprised and quickly opened the door. She hugged me lovingly and kissed my cheek. She had never displayed this affection before. In fact I was meeting her after a long time. I made her comfortable and over a cup of tea Reena told me that Ayesha had come to visit her at the clinic. My heart missed a beat, so that is why she is here in Mumbai! "Sukriti I am so happy. I cannot tell you how happy you have made me. Dada is going to be a father, after so many years of disappointment, but I am also afraid; very afraid for both of you." Reena was both crying and laughing.

This touched my frayed nerves and I began to weep bitterly, telling her my apprehensions about Ashwin not believing me, after all he had been convinced that he cannot father a child; I also told her that I was going to have the baby at the cost of the honor of my family and my career. Reena was apprehensive about the repercussions it would have on my life, "Sukriti are you bold enough to face the consequences of such a step?" Reena had tried to make me see reason; I know she was a well meaning friend who genuinely cared for me. She portrayed a fearful picture of future for me, but seeing my determination; she gave in and embraced me promising to be by my side all through this. "I have not told Dada yet. Like you I also feel that Dada will find it difficult to accept the fact considering his situation. But everything will be alright. At least mummy will be happy," Reena went on.

"Reena, this is not a normal situation. Your brother is a married man, he is a public figure, and we must not disclose this to anyone. As far as I am concerned, I will not associate Ashwin with any of these. This is my decision and I alone will face the consequences. Do you understand Reena, the need to be discreet? We have to consider the feelings of his wife also. Why should she suffer humiliation because of this? Please promise me you will not tell this to anyone, not to your mother also," I requested Reena.

"But how will you face the people, your family, and your colleagues, alone? What will you tell them about the father of your child, be practical, the child needs a father as much as a mother," Reena argued.

"Do you anticipate the scandal, the public outcry if your brother's name is involved in this?" I tried to reason out with Reena. We argued and discussed the matter a great length and finally decided to tell nobody about the baby till my pregnancy was visible, and then I would announce my pregnancy without divulging the name of the father. "Let the people make their own conjectures." I had the right to silence and I would go away to some place to have the baby and stay there till the people had forgotten the whole incident. Ashwin will be told in the due course of time. It seemed so simple and easy after that.

Ashwin was calling me regularly getting desperate to meet, threatening that he was going to land at my apartment any day, if I did not plan some meeting soon. "How about staying for a few days in Chahal in the same cottage?" he asked one day. I knew it was risky for me to travel in this condition to a hill station. I made excuses, citing reasons of office work, the meetings; in exasperation he stopped asking and his nightly calls became irregular. Although this made me miserable, I had no choice. Reema was calling me many times a day, suggesting medicine, precautions and rest. She was proving to be very helpful. Her calls lifted my spirits, Ayesha was also calling me, encouraging me to be brave. At time like this I used to call myself fortunate for having such friends.

That day I had completed the fifth month of my pregnancy, at night Reena called up, she sounded tense, her husband had overheard our conversation earlier in the day on the telephone extension and he had forced Reena to tell him the whole truth. He had stormed out of the house and not returned so far. "He is not even answering my call," she said anxiously.

"Don't worry he will come home, he must be hurt that you have concealed such a fact from him," I tried to pacify her. I was worried, what would Dr. Sadanand do! Confront Ashwin! Tell him! Oh no God! I don't want Ashwin to know this way.

Next day I was feeling unwell and I called up my office to report sick leave. I lay in bed; my maid gave me some tea. I slept the whole day. In my sleep I dreamt that Ashwin was sitting by my bedside watching me, late in the evening I woke up and called my maid for some water. To my surprise it was Ashwin who handed me a glass of water; the shock was so intense that I nearly dropped the glass from my hand. He held the glass to my lips and made me drink some water. He did not speak a word but kept looking at my face. I felt terribly nervous, as I lay against my pillows my eyes closed, waiting for his angry tirade. But nothing came, no word. I opened my eyes and saw Ashwin sitting in the chair tears falling down his cheek. He was weeping. With great difficulty I sat up and took his hands in mine and kissed them. He put his arms around me and we both began to sob.

Later on when we had recovered our composure he told me that the news of my pregnancy came as a shock, "as if a thunder bolt had struck me. I was in the office when Sadanand came barging in and began to blast me. First I did not understand what he was accusing me of. Later on when he told me about your condition, my initial reaction was shock, but then I knew in the inner recess of my heart that it was true, it is my child, Sukriti ! This is our child! You have nothing to fear, I am with you at every step of the way." He put his protective arms around me, "My darling, why did you not tell me this yourself? You kept making excuses about not meeting me, I began to get insecure. So this was it. You were hiding this news all these months. Sadanand was telling me you are already in the sixth month of your pregnancy. Is that so?" He was like a small boy enthusiastic about something that had been long denied to him.

"Ashwin, you know I love you and now our love has become more binding for us. But we have to face facts. You have a wife, a career, public obligation and your family to consider. One impulsive step will destroy them all and more so your wife. Openly coming out with the declaration that it is your child, will prove disastrous for you. I will also face censure, family ostracism, perhaps lose my job, but beyond that nothing more will happen to me. I will live through this and the thought of my child will make me stronger. You have a lot at stake. So don't take any step, now just be happy in the thought that your child is safe and being loved and cared for, by its mother. Sooner or later I will have to disclose my pregnancy and I am ready to face anything. But you stay away from this; let me handle this in my own way. Please do what I tell you," I spoke in a calm voice;

I had to be stronger of the two. I could see Ashwin was struggling to keep his emotions in check. He heard me patiently. "I am so proud of you, but we are in this together. I will talk to Radhika, tell her the truth and if she accepts the situation good for her or else she will have to live all her life with her lies. Tomorrow I will meet Bhaskar uncle and put in my resignation from the cabinet, party and my membership. For me nothing is more important than you and our child. We will go away to some peaceful place in the hills. I want to be with you through all this and stand proudly by your side as our child enters the world," Ashwin went on; it all must have seemed so easy for him at that moment. Next day when he left my flat to catch an early morning flight, he left all his contact numbers, "Just in case you need, I am just a call away, my darling." He kissed me lingeringly possessively touching my now visible bulging waist. Then he was gone.

Reena called me during the day while I was working in the office and told me that Ashwin had gone to meet Ma who lived on Ashram Road in a bungalow in Delhi, she liked to live alone and had three old trusted servants being looked after. Reena and Sadanand were also called there and in their presence he had told his mother about me and my pregnancy and his decision to resign. Reena told me, "Ma took all this revelation calmly. She had suspected all along that something was wrong with his marriage. Ma told Dada that he had every right to live his life in the way he liked but he has obligation towards his wife. His child and the child's mother are also his responsibility, but Radhika should not be humiliated. He should have consideration for the feeling of his wife also".

Reena told me that Ma had not spoken to Ashwin after that but "went to her room refusing to come out even when we went to take her leave" I was not dismayed, I knew my father would also react in the same way. I had to take a decision sooner or later.

That night I told Mr. Mallingam that I was coming over to his house for dinner and wanted to eat the delicious South Indian food Mrs. Mallingam was so famous for. I had decided that I will disclose my pregnancy to them at their house in homily surroundings. Ever since I had come to Mumbai ten years back, this loving couple had been my guardian angels. I knew in them I will always have a shoulder to lean on.

I reached their house situated on Carter Road. It was an old British bungalow with an open stretch of land; such spacious houses are now rare in Mumbai. Mrs. Savitha Mallingam was a graceful lady of around sixty years. I was touched by the warm welcome she gave me. She was surprised to see me in a sari and commented that my skin was glowing. Later on in the evening after a delicious South Indian dinner, we sat out in the balcony sipping Mrs. Mallingam's home grounded coffee. It was the appropriate time to break the news. "Savitha Ma'am, I have come here on some personal business . . . I . . . I am six months pregnant and I have decided to have the baby." I said it hurriedly and waited to see their reaction; there was none from Mr. Mallingam, five decades of journalistic career had trained him to mask his feelings well, although Mrs. Mallingam's eyes opened wide and then hastily looked away. Mr. Mallingam at last spoke, "Wish to speak about it?"

"There is nothing much to say, except that I am in love with the father of my child but we are caught in peculiar situation and cannot legalize our relationship," I said briefly.

"Surely Sukriti the man must feel some kind of responsibility towards you and your child. You cannot go through this alone!" Mrs. Mallingam had recovered by now.

"Ma'am, he is with me every step of the way. But he holds a certain position. This will cause the biggest ever scandal and I want to spare him the embarrassment," I said.

'Ahem' was Mr. Mallingam's reaction. Mrs. Mallingam thought I had gone crazy, "What kind of love is it! Is he married?" Seeing my nod, she fell silent and we remained silent for a long time. Finally I had to say something. "So what I want to say is that I will be resigning from my job as soon as you find some replacement for me. If you wish to tell our colleagues about it, it is alright with me because I am not ashamed of my condition, but I am sorry if I am causing you embarrassment."

"No, not at all, Sukriti, I am a broad minded man. Your story has brought back the long forgotten memories of my youth. But never mind, there is no need for you to resign. We are living in a metropolitan city, such things are accepted here. So go on with your work. But tell me when you are due and I will sanction you the maternity leave with all monetary benefits. Anyway congratulations," he said.

Afterwards no words were spoken about my condition. In fact Mrs. Mallingam was so caring that she packed a variety of her home made pickles and sauces in various jars and urged me to have them whenever I had felt the desire. "When I was expecting Gauri I must have devoured bottles of mango pickles," she said and hugged me lovingly. When I took leave she advised me to wear low heel sandals and to take regular exercise. I came home feeling cheerful. One front had been successfully tackled. Now my family had to be dealt with.

That night I called my eldest sister Suhasini in Kodaicanal. She had always treated me like her daughter; there was ten years of age difference between us. I told her about my pregnancy and repeated the words I had told Mr. and Mrs. Maliingam using the same tone. Her reaction was shock, then tears, anger, calling me a slur on the name of the family. Finally her anger subsided and she inquired of my health parameters. Being a doctor; a gynecologist, she asked me various questions, prescribed me some vitamin capsules and before disconnecting she became emotional, "Sukriti, my child, please marry this man. The child needs the mother and the father." How very typical of my sister. In spite of being so highly qualified and having travelled extensively, she was a very traditional woman and my South Indian brother-in-law, a doctor himself was always at the receiving end of her fetish for customs. She was only afraid of her daughter. As expected within a period of two hours I received a frantic call from my second sister, Sabi who was a professor of Psychology in the Marthwada University in Aurangabad. Married to a software engineer, Sabi was an unconventional lady. She had been quite a beauty while in college. My brothers Ajay and Ganesh had to spy on her to see whether she was going to the college or to meet one of her admirers. They had heaved sigh of relief when Anshul's parents had brought a marriage proposal for her. Sabi had insisted that she will first meet the boy, get to know him better and then give her consent. Anshul had indulged all her whims in the two months of courtship period that finally she had given her 'yes' to marriage. Now they had two children and were still very much in love. Sabi had been given the news by Suhasini.

Sabi was serious when she talked to me and in her own subtle way tried to drive some sense in my 'silly head'. She pleaded, "Suku, have you thought how you are going to bring up the child alone? Who is the father? Why he cannot marry you?" Sabi had so many questions to ask me. I could see that she was upset it made me feel bad. I realized that it was their love for me that was making them frantic. In the end Anshul Bhai took the phone from her and spoke to me in his calm voice that I should not mind Sabi's anger and she was upset and in due course of time she will come around, but I should take care of myself. "I will talk to you later." He disconnected. Then it was Ganesh and later Ajay, the same questions, anger, and emotions. Ultimately they all felt defeated.

I was surprised my father did not speak to me. Perhaps he was not told. I felt terribly sorry about all this. I know it was very difficult for my family to accept this situation. We are a middle class family with middle class values of modesty, legal relationships and legitimacy. I must have caused deep pain to them, because after that day my brothers did not call me but my darling sisters Suhasini and Sabi were calling me every day dropping hints about marriage, wanting to know the identity of the man, but all the same they assured me that they loved me and they would be with me when I needed them. Suhasini and her husband Srinivas were urging me to come to Kodaicanal, where they will take good care of me. My reserved brother-in-law also suggested that they will adopt the child and that way I will always have access to my child. I was touched by their concern and promised to think it over.

My colleagues at the newspaper office were told about my pregnancy by Mr. Mallingam. He had called the heads of the different departments to his office for an informal meeting and towards the end of the meeting he made the announcement about my pregnancy. Hush fell over the people but soon they recovered and congratulated me. Mr. Mallingam suggested that they can break the news to their department subordinates in any way they liked, "But," he warned, "No gossip, no character assassination. We must respect Sukriti's Privacy." It was quite easy. No one asked me, I was not answerable to anyone. In fact all my subordinates became very protective towards me and I was enjoying every moment of my pregnancy.

Reena was calling me every day giving me medical tips; Suhasini, Sabi, their families were all concerned. One day my father called me late at night. His voice was calm when he told me that he had been told by Ajay and his wife about my condition. It had no doubt "shocked "him but he had now recovered. He did not ask me any questions and told me that I should take care of myself. "Suhasini and Sabi will be there with you. Don't worry about people, if you are happy so am I," he said. Tears welled in my eyes. His calm acceptance was so humbling for me. My father was like that never interfering in the lives of his children, he believed that parents should gently guide their grown up children and leave them free to live life on their own terms. I thanked him and promised to call him.

Nanu called me from Srinagar. Poor Nanu had gone so senile with age that she kept asking me when I had got married. I had no heart to tell her the facts. Perhaps Suhasini may have told her about my pregnancy and not about my marital status. Nanu talked of her apples and pears, and her aches and pains. I realized that it was not safe for her to stay alone in that house but despite the pleadings of my father and sisters she had stubbornly refused to come and live with them saying, "I had come to this house as a seventeen year old bride, I will leave for my eternal abode from this house only."

Ashwin was calling me many times during the day, worried sick about my being alone. I was nearing the ninth month of my pregnancy and had become too heavy to move around freely. My blood pressure was on the higher side and doctor had advised me complete bed rest or hospitalization.

Around this time the film of my friend Surinder Katoch was released and for the second time my story was appreciated. The film and the story received rave reviews. People's interest in me was aroused again. The media was hounding me and I was not going to appear before it in my present condition. Some over enthusiastic reporters had seen me visiting a nursing home, they smelt some juicy story for their gossip columns and sure enough what followed, was a full blown picture of me with my bulging belly and the caption "Elusive novelist and journalist traced in a nursing home" and there were articles about my pregnancy, many conjectures about my marital status, the guess work, who the father could be. Once it was confirmed to the media that I was not married, they had a field day tearing my character to shreds. The vernacular press called it 'moral depravity'. Another so-called progressive channel invented some stories and flashed the old photograph where I was shown being embraced by a popular cine star with the caption 'Could this be the man!' Poor actor was married. Some people who had only a brief acquaintance with me were being called for interviews; they claimed a close friendship with me and hinted at my bohemian lifestyle. There were reporters standing near my office building to click me. The more popular the film became, the lower my character fell, thanks to the paparazzi.

But that gem of a man, Mr. Mallingam stood firmly by my side whenever I suggested I should not come to office. "No, they are doing their work, you do your work" was the simple logic he would tell me. Ashwin was getting terribly disturbed by all this. He could not even come and meet me because there seemed to be a constant stream of reporters posted in the vicinity of my apartment. He would often tell me in extreme frustration, "You are suffering alone. Let me speak up or let's go away Sukriti. Let's go abroad. I have many friends who will shelter us. We can live happily together there." I would laugh it all and call him chicken hearted.

The fact was that this clamour was unnerving me also. My sisters were getting disturbed; their friends and in-laws were questioning them about me. I heard Ganesh had beaten up a journalist who had asked him about the father of my child. What sadistic pleasure the media was getting out of this! I could only guess that it raised their TRP. One day Mr. Mallingam suggested that I call a press conference in the press club or give a statement "Maybe they will leave you in peace after this." So invitations were sent out and on the day of the conference I was at the club looking calm and calculated and Mr. Mallingam by my side. I welcomed all my friends, thanked them for the coverage they were giving me since many days. I confirmed their doubts about my pregnancy telling them that yes indeed I was in the family way but I did not want to disclose the name of the father at this point of time and in due course of time I will announce his name. I took a few more questions and then left the venue.

Mr. Mallingam was wrong; the media had now taken over itself to find this mystery man. There were many theories built up, some even dragged the name of poor Mr. Mallingam also, much to my embarrassment. But he laughed at it, praising the fertile brains of journalists. He called it 'The theory of probability'. The peace that I needed at this stage of pregnancy was denied to me. Ashwin would tell me how he and his wife were constantly quarrelling over minor issues; Radhika was upset to see that her husband was spending more time out of the house. Ashwin had confided to me that he used to work in his office till late hours and only turn in once the whole household was asleep. She had even complained about it to Ashwin's mother. Poor Ma had only looked on helplessly not knowing whose side to take. Ashwin was getting desperate; he wanted to find an end to this dual life he was leading. He even suggested to Radhika that since there was so much tension between them, they should try living separately; this alarmed her so much that she went to Bhaskar Uncle and complained that Ashwin was thinking of leaving her. Ashwin told me that Bhaskar uncle had come to Ma's house one night over for dinner and called Ashwin there. A heated argument had taken place between the two over Ashwin's treatment of Radhika. Ashwin had told him the truth without disclosing my identity, Ashwin had begged him to let him resign and quit his seat and the party. "I want to live in peace and bring up my child" Ashwin pleaded with his uncle. Bhaskar uncle heard him then left promising to think over the matter. Ashwin had felt relieved that at least his whole family knew about me and his yet to be born child.

I had a strong hunch that this will not come to a happy ending. My sympathy was with Radhika and there were moments of self-reproach and guilt that I was responsible for her unhappiness. If only I had been strong and resisted Ashwin's love our situation would have been different, who knows we may have been happy in our separate worlds.

CHAPTER 9

Two weeks had passed since Ashwin had disclosed the truth to his uncle. One day I was in the office working at my desk, Philomena, my personal assistant called on the intercom to say that a gentleman, Mr. Sharan wanted to meet me urgently. "He says it is a private meeting." I was intrigued but all the same told him to send him in. Mr. Sharan was an elderly gentleman with a kind face. He introduced himself as a social worker. I thought he wanted me to do an article on him and his work. But no, he had been sent by Mr. Bhaskar. I was taken aback Ashwin had told me that he had not disclosed my identity to his uncle. Mr. Sharan asked for my forgiveness for coming without an appointment, "but it is urgent and if you would be kind enough to come down with me to the parking lot because Mr. Bhaskar is in the car. He wishes to see you." I found it hard to believe, this must be some ploy, I might get abducted. I had to use my common sense. I said, "Mr. Bhaskar, you say, has something urgent to discuss with me, he can meet me in our conference room. Nobody will see him there or hear our conversation. Please bring him to the fourth floor and there the security will show you the place, I will join you in a moment," I said. To my surprise, Mr. Sharan went out of the office.

Later on when I enquired from the security officer in the fourth floor if there were any persons asking for me, he said there were two elderly gentlemen in the waiting room. I came down from my office to the fourth floor, conference hall. My legs were shaking; it seemed all like a dream, what does he want? I was sure it was something to do with my relationship with Ashwin. I could have called Ashwin while coming down, told him about it but something stopped me, I did not want to cause him worry. As I entered the room, I recognized Mr. Bhaskar. During the early days of my career, I had done a few interviews of him. He was then an MP and had shown flashes of great wit and leadership.

Mr. Sharan left the room and I greeted Mr. Bhaskar respectfully, I bent down to touch his feet, he put out his hand by way of blessings. I ordered water and some tea. He said nothing but kept watching my movements. We were silent and only the ticking of the clock could be heard. I was mentally preparing myself for his censure, his anger and even his denunciation of me, but to my surprise he spoke softly and gently. "May I call you by your name? Yes! That is better. So Sukriti I will come directly to the purpose of my visit. You are not surprised by my visit which means you are aware that I know the truth. I should be congratulating you and my nephew on your happiness. But the circumstances are such that I will have to withhold my words," he paused. I did not say anything I kept looking at the ground and waited him to say whatever he had to. At that time I was beyond feeling anything. Even if he had threatened me or cursed me I would have taken it all without any bitterness. "Do you realize what this will do to Ashwin ! Destroy him and destroy me. It would be what you term it in your journalistic jargon 'Sex Scandal'. A minister of his stature having a child with his mistress! He is being seen as my successor, one who will take over the reins of the party in few years time. Do you want to see him groveling in the dust? Think over it?" He said there was no anger in his voice just regret. "My nephew is ready to give up everything for you. And one day he will blame you for all this. There is nothing more intoxicating than power. Ashwin is used to adulation, command; tell me can he stay out of this forever? Once this thing is out in public domain he will be finished. You can see how the media is clamoring about you. Same will happen to him."

I could see he was right, the same arguments I had given Ashwin. Mr. Bhaskar's words did not hurt me but they made a lot of sense. I heard him in silence. When he had finished, he stood up and I also stood up, he came closer to me and put both his hands on my shoulder, his voice was choking with controlled emotions, "Sukriti forgive me for hurting you. He is like a son to me. I cannot let him ruin his future, much as I want to see him happy. You can help him, now you have to decide what he should do." He left the room and I quietly took the elevator to get back to my office.

I am not a person to wallow in self-pity. That night I made up my mind that I will have to have a hard talk with Ashwin even if it hurt him. I called him up at midnight because that was the time he was alone in the office and could speak freely. I did not tell him about his uncle's visit. But gave him my decision to sever all ties with him and he need not call me again. I am using this expression to narrate that I gave him no opportunity to explain, to plead. I told him that I was going away to Kodaicanal to live with my sister Suhasini and the baby will be born there. He should not call me, and if he did try to meet me or call me I will kill myself and the baby. This was all so baffling for him. The more he pleaded with me the harder I became and in the end banged the phone and switched off all my cell phones.

I wanted to be left in peace. I had had enough. I cooked my dinner, had my medicine and sat down to take stock of my situation. I will need someone to be with me in the hospital. Going to Suhasini was not in my contemplation, she was used to having her way that would make me miserable. Sabi had her own children to look after. To my bad luck Ayesha had received a scholarship to pursue her post-doctoral degree in London School of Economics. Anyway I still had Mrs. Mallingam; she would not let me down. I will stay here, till the baby was born then leave Mumbai for some quiet place. With these plans I fell asleep.

Next one week went in daze. Ashwin called me several times during those days sending me messages to at least pick up the phone. He was wondering whether I had gone to Kodaicanal. He had tried calling my office but I had instructed all my staff that my whereabouts were not to be disclosed to anybody. For the first time in all these months I was thinking clearly. I was determined to face the situation boldly without anybody's support.

The day of my delivery was approaching; doctor had told me to check into the hospital as soon as I felt cramps in my lower abdomen. I had kept a bag ready with baby's stuff. I was not nervous; in fact I was feeling much better and peaceful. One day much to my disbelief, I had a visit from Dr. Sadanand; Reena's husband at my office. He appeared suddenly and stood before me as I was getting into the elevator to come down. He put his hand on my shoulder which nearly frightened me. He must have seen surprise on my face, he quickly said, "I have not come as an emissary of Ashwin but as your friend and well-wisher. Forget that I am related to him. I have come on my own and nobody knows about it, not even Reena. So relax." I had met him once or twice, I liked him. He seemed a straight forward man.

I took him to the coffee house situated in the ground floor of my office building. As soon as we ordered coffee, he began "Sukriti, I have thought over this matter and I greatly admire you for your firm stand. Ashwin is in shock, but he will recover. You have every right to live your life the way you want, decide whether you want to be known as somebody's mistress all your life. Now the question is your impending confinement, care after delivery and the upbringing of the child. Mumbai will not be suitable place for this purpose. Leave it as soon as the baby is born and you are strong enough to travel. May I suggest something, let Reena help you. I promise you Ashwin or anybody will know nothing about this arrangement. Everything will be managed discreetly. We will rent a comfortable house for you away from the humdrum of this life. You can stay there as long as you like. If you want any member of your family to stay with you, you can call them," he said and waited for my response. His words were sinking in and I admired the clarity of his thinking.

"I have lived in Dalhousie in Himachal Pradesh for few years during my school days and the place has always fascinated me. I would like to live there; can you arrange some house for me? After my delivery I will go away quietly and settle down there. I have enough savings they will last me for few years. Once I have some help with the baby, I will resume my writing. I already have a novel ready for publication. That should bring me decent earnings." Surprisingly I found myself trusting him and speaking freely.

He was impressed. He assured me that everything will be arranged smoothly, Reena was to accompany me from Mumbai to Dalhousie, without anyone knowing about it. Once I was settled in the new place Reena will return to Delhi. She will stay in touch with me. Before leaving Sadanand gave me a brotherly hug and said, "You and your baby are my moral responsibility. Remember Reena and I will always be by your side whenever you need us." I felt blessed that I had wonderful people as my friends, my sisters loved me and my father understood my needs. What more could I have asked for!

That night my water bag burst and I understood it was sign of labor. I called Mr. Mallingam, He and his wife reached my apartment within one hour and drove me to the hospital. I was in labour for the remaining part of the night. Pains were intense; Mrs. Mallingam held my hand, urging me to push with all my strength, the doctor, the nurses all stood by me. At five minutes to six in the morning my Nikki was born a chubby, red-faced baby, with a frown upon her brows. Mrs. Mallingam told me, 'a beautiful baby girl just like you,' as she put the bundle in my arms. I had read and heard the ecstasy a new mother feels when she holds her new born for the first time in her arms. I could feel love gushing out of my breasts there were tears in my eyes as I held her tightly to my bosom. She did not resemble me, but had an uncanny resemblance to her aunt Reena. A tiny mole on her left cheek at the same spot as Reena has. I marveled at the powers of genes.

Later in the day, I called Reena to give the news, she began to sob and could not speak coherently, and Sadanand quickly took the phone from her and congratulated me. "Reena is crying with joy," he teased. When I told him that the baby was a replica of Reena he was overjoyed, he said that now he is happy that he has a daughter too. Before disconnecting he told me that all the arrangements had been done and gave me the detailed plan of my leaving Mumbai. I called up Suhasini and Sabi giving them the news, there were sniffs, tears, congratulations and both my sisters wanted to come to Mumbai to be with me. I convinced them that I was in good hands; my friends were with me and taking good care of me. "What about the father of the child?" Suhasini was curious. "He is by my bedside taking care of me. Don't worry about anything," I said and hung up.

My father called me later in the afternoon, he said that Suhasini had given him the news and he hoped the child and I were both well. He told me that the child was born on a very auspicious day, it being 'Poornima', the fifteenth day of the moon, considered to be a holy day when many Hindus fast. He had consulted the 'Panchang', the Hindu calendar book, my daughter was born under the influence of Rohini star which he told me was also the birth star of Lord Krishna.

"Sukriti, your daughter will bring you fame and commendations," my father said and gave me and my baby lots of blessings. He did not ask me about my future plans or the man responsible for my baby's birth but asked me if I had everything I and the infant needed. My dear father was like that. I remember when I was in college and often spent a lot of time in the library and came home late, my mother used to get angry with me and tell my father that he was not disciplining us enough. He would tell her, "Parents should protect the baby, guide the child, and leave the adult free; otherwise they will never inculcate the sense of responsibility for their actions." My mother would grumble some more and give in.

I stayed in the hospital for four days. The doctors had shielded me from any kind of public access, only Mr. and Mrs. Mallingam were allowed to visit me. On the fifth day, I left the hospital late at night, accompanied by Mrs. Mallingam. I stayed the night in my apartment and the next night Reena arrived and accompanied me to Dalhousie.

CHAPTER 10

Nikki whimpered in her sleep and I heard someone speaking loudly, oh! I had again been thinking of the past. The air hostess was making the announcement about the plane landing at Palam airport in a short while. I quickly fastened Nikki's seat belt and my own. Nikki was now wide awake. She was smiling. "Darling how is your ear?" I kissed her on her curly head. As she was growing her resemblance to Reena was becoming more noticeable, the curly hair, sharp nose, light colored eyes and the little mole on the left cheek. I used to often tease Reena, "She looks more like your daughter than mine." Reena doted on her niece and whenever she would come to Dalhousie she would bring bags full of clothes and toys for her. "It is not paining anymore? Are we about to land?" Nikki asked, she had a clear expression at her age. She was an inquisitive child, asking questions about things she saw for the first time. I would answer all her questions patiently and sit for hours with her telling her stories, singing songs, and playing doll house with her. From all accounts I could call my life busy and contented.

I was visiting Delhi for the first time after four years, in fact I had not gone out of Dalhousie since the day I had arrived here with five days old Nikki in my arms many years. Reema had insisted that I should come to Delhi to have Nikki's ear seen by a famous ENT specialist, because Nikki was often complaining about pain in the left ear. Reena had told me that she also had suffered from leaking ear when she was small and had to have an operation to cure this. She had warned me that if it is neglected, the pus may reach the brain or impair the hearing. So I had decided to meet this ENT in Delhi and go back to Dalhousie quickly.

Sadanand was waiting for me at the airport. He hugged me and Nikki, I am always happy to see him. We drove straight to the hotel where Sadanand had made arrangement for us for two days. I had agreed to come to Delhi on the condition that I will not stay at Reena's house. It would be too painful for me, there would be her servants, and I did not wish to make myself noticeable. Sadanand left us at the hotel.

Later that afternoon Reena and her son Vishu visited us. Vishu, whom I was seeing after five years, was now a strapping young man. He was happy to see Nikki. Reena had not told him anything about his relationship with Nikki. Vishu was observing Nikki very carefully and then commented, "Mummy she also has a mole on her left cheek like yours." Reena looked at me. In the evening Reena took us to the ENT specialist situated at Cannaught Place. The doctor examined Nikki's ear for a long time and suggested a minor surgery to prevent the infection from spreading. I needed time to think over. I did not think it wise to prolong my stay in this city. Back in the hotel I was in two minds whether to go through the operation or go back to Dalhousie. The doctor had said that I should not wait for too long.

Next day I had made up my mind that the operation would be done and I will extend my visit by another week. I called up the doctor and he fixed the operation for the evening that day. He assured me that it was a minor surgery and will be over in half an hour and Nikki will be discharged in two days' time. I called up Reena and she came to pick us up in the evening.

On the way I kept talking to Nikki, telling her how the doctor would see her ear and she would not feel anything. She was frightened and sat in my lap throughout the drive. When the nurse came to take her to the changing room, she became nervous and started crying. I held her close to me, trying to pacify her, she could not be pacified. Her crying attracted the attention of other patients in the wards. It was visiting time. There was quite crowd of visitors.

I saw a familiar face coming out one of the wards, it was Radhika. She saw Reena first and came towards her, and then she saw me with the bawling child in my arms. Radhika recognized me and nodded in my direction and exchanged greetings with Reena. And she was the last person I would have wanted to meet at this point of time. I always felt a twinge of guilt thinking about her. I quietly went into the changing room with Nikki

The surgery took just half an hour to be completed while Reena and I stood outside the operation theatre pacing around. Reena told me that Radhika was asking about Nikki. Reena had told her about her ear problem. Radhika was visiting one of her aunts who had just had hearing device implanted in her ear.

Nikki was still semiconscious when she was wheeled out of the OT. The doctor told me that she would come around in one hour. She was under sedatives and I should let her sleep. My little girl looked pale as she slept. Tears filled my eyes as I watched her wincing in pain. Sadanand and Vishu also came to the hospital. Reena insisted that she will stay with me in the hospital that night. I could not refuse; as a matter of fact I did not want to be alone that night. I wanted someone near me, to assure me that my baby was going to be alright. We stayed awake, watching over Nikki for any signs of discomfort but she slept, although fitfully.

At around 2 a.m. that night I felt a gentle knock at the door of our room. The sound came again, Reena called out, it was the nurse who had come to check on Nikki, and behind her was Reena's mother followed by Ashwin. I was dumbfounded as they entered the room. I began to shake violently, "Oh my God, this is what I had been avoiding all these years." Meeting him at here and that too when I was in no condition to defend myself against his anger. The irony of our situation struck me hard. He looked old and thin

Ma looked at me briefly and then headed straight for Nikki's bed. Ashwin stood rooted at the doorstep undecided, I was feeling terribly weak. I thought I would fall but supported myself against the wall. How . . . why . . . why have they come, who told him about us? My mind was not in a state to think straight. Reena was equally surprised but she recovered quickly and told Ma about Nikki's operation.

Ma was watching Nikki as if mesmerized. She gently touched her hair and bent down to kiss her forehead; tears were trickling down her cheeks as she hastily wiped them away with the edge of her saree. Ashwin moved and walked towards Nikki. He did not even once look at me. He stood near his mother and watched Nikki. I was too afraid to even look at him. I saw him bend down and touch the small hand of his daughter. His mother put her arm around his back and then something strange happened; mother and the son were weeping. Reena went to them and comforted Ashwin. I stood apart, the only outsider in that small circle of blood relations. I went out of the ward with shaking legs and sat in the chair in the corridor.

I had no doubt in my mind that Radhika must have mentioned meeting Reena in the hospital with her 'journalist friend'. I don't know how long I must have sat there, when Reena came running to me that Nikki was calling for me. I rushed into the room. Ashwin and his mother were still standing near Nikki's bed and she was crying. I sat on the bed and half lying with her I gathered her in my arms. She was moaning softly in pain. I kept talking to her, telling her the nice things we will do when she was better. In my maternal impulse I had become oblivious to the presence of Ma and Ashwin. They watched silently. At one point Nikki opened her eyes wide and saw ma looking down at her, she asked me, "Who is she Mama?" I did not answer but Ma said, "I am your grandmother." God knows what Nikki heard; she smiled and closed her eyes. Soon she was asleep and I got up softly from the bed.

Reena forced Ma and Ashwin to sit down. I stood near the window looking out, my back towards them, this was the shock of my life; a situation that I could have never anticipated. Finally Ma stood up, came up to me and put her hand on my shoulder. I was surprised by her gesture. She made me sit on the spare bed and sat next to me. Ashwin and Reena watched. Ma took my hand in her hands and said in a choked voice, "I am sorry Sukriti. My son has caused you a great pain. You have done our family a favour by giving us a grandchild." I did not answer and kept my eyes down. She went on, "I had thought I will die without seeing my grandchild. But God's ways are strange, how he brought you and my granddaughter here! All this is destiny. You and I cannot run away from this." Ma paused and stood up to see Nikki again. I could see that the sight of her granddaughter was so overwhelming that she was irresistibly getting drawn to her. I suppose blood has a magnetic pull.

At last I looked around and saw Ashwin looking at me. When our eyes met he did not turn away but held my gaze. All his hair had turned grey; he looked older and the expression in his eyes was sad. He had not spoken a word till then. He cleared his throat and spoke to me, "You have punished me enough by keeping me away from my daughter." I was about to retort when Reena sensing confrontation building up between us, hastily intervened to diffuse the situation. She began to tell Ashwin how well Nikki had behaved during and after the operation. Ashwin was angry with both of us. He told Reena, "You, my own sister; also deceived me. You were with her all these years and did not even tell me. You also helped Sukriti to keep my child away from me."

Reena kept quiet, Ma said, "It is nobody's fault Ashwin. Both of them did this to protect your reputation and save your marriage. Bhaskar told me recently about his meeting with Sukriti in her office and what had transpired there." Ma came to me and said, "Forgive us." After this nobody spoke and finally Ma said that they should leave now because both Reena and I needed some rest. She literally dragged Ashwin from the room. I urged Reena to go home because she had a working day at the clinic. I assured her that there would be no problem. Nikki was sleeping and I will also sleep for a little while. She went reluctantly.

I tried to sleep but the events of the night kept haunting me. I was still in a state of shock, it was like a dream from where I would wake up any time. I tried to fathom my feelings for Ashwin, did I still love him? I was confused and spent the night thinking about it. I knew my peace had once again been shattered. It would be a long time before I will be able to live a normal life again.

Next day the doctor told me that Nikki was well on the way of recovery and I could take her home in the evening. I had a bath and changed into a pair of jeans and loose T-shirt. Nikki was fully awake and a bit cranky so I sat on the bed cradling her in my arms and singing her favorite song 'my little darling'. I had composed this song for her when she was very small, she liked it so much that she would often tell me to sing this for her. I kept stroking her hair. There was a knock at the door. Ma entered wearing an elegant cotton saree of white colour followed by her driver carrying a big Tiffin box in one hand and another bulging bag slung from his shoulder. Ma came straight towards us and patted Nikki's head. Nikki was looking at her intently and said, "I have seen you before." Ma smiled and said, "Yes, you saw me yesterday." They both hit it off immediately and soon enough I was sitting on the chair and Ma was lying on Nikki's bed holding her in her arms and telling her some story. I was watching them and felt happy that at least Ma was having some happiness with her grandchild after having waited for this so long.

I must have fallen asleep and woke up when I heard some soft voices. I opened my eyes with a start and I saw Ashwin sitting on the bed and cradling Nikki in his arms and Ma was sitting on the stool near the bed. Nikki had put her head on Ashwin's chest and was laughing at some joke. The scene was so touching that I had no heart to disturb it. So I closed my eyes again pretending to be fast asleep. I heard Ma saying, "Ashu, I better wake her up for lunch. She might not have eaten anything since yesterday." Ashwin's voice, "Let her sleep Ma, she must have been awake whole night, see how pale she is looking." I could detect concern in Ashwin's voice. So he was not angry with me! "Thanks to Radhika for telling me that she had met Reena in the hospital with her journalist friend. Radhika had called me to say that she was leaving for London on some conference and will not be coming for my birthday and she casually mentioned meeting Reena and her friend. I put two and two together and immediately called you," Ma was talking to Ashwin. So it was Ma who had brought him there!

I heard him say, "Ma I would never have found her and Nikki, just imagine Reena was in it throughout and pretended that she had no clue about Sukriti, she knew all about Sukriti and Nikki." I heard Nikki speaking, "You are talking about my Mamma. How do you know my Mamma's name?" Ashwin said lovingly, "Because your Mumma is my . . ." and then Reena arrived and he could not complete his sentence. What he was going to say, I wondered.

I opened my eyes and pretended surprise at Ashwin's presence. Ma told Reena to serve lunch. She had brought enough food to feed all of us. Even Ashwin ate heartily but we did not talk directly to each other. I fed a little food to Nikki who was sitting in Ashwin's lap all along and I found it awkward to sit so close to him while feeding Nikki but he did not seem to mind and coaxed Nikki to eat some more. Reena and Ma were smiling indulgently. Ma commented, "Ashu look what a striking resemblance she has with Reena." Ashwin said, "Ma this is the marvel of genes." Nikki asked in all innocence, "You mean the jeans we wear?" Ashwin in his serious tone began to explain to her about genes. At one point Nikki called him 'uncle', he looked up sharply at me and told her to call him 'Baba'. "I am your Baba," he explained to her, "And she is Badi Ma," pointing towards Ma. I was enjoying this family scene and also regretting that tomorrow all this will be over and we will all be in separate worlds.

That evening Nikki was discharged from the hospital and Sadanand, Reena and Ma urged me to leave the hotel and shift to Reena's house. "Nikki will have better care under two doctors," Ma told me, "Please do listen to me," Ma said almost pleading with me. I did not have the heart to disappoint her. I agreed to shift to Reena's house for the remaining days of my stay.

Ma also came to live with us. Nikki was enjoying the attention she was getting. Ma was spoiling her thoroughly with love and gifts. Sadanand, Reena and Vishu had found a new baby and could not leave her out of sight. Reena had asked me if I had any objections to Ashwin visiting the house to see Nikki. I could not deny a father the right to see his child, I had already done a lot of damage, but I had warned Reena that Nikki should not know that Ashwin was her father. It will disturb her life. Reena agreed with me and conveyed my feelings to Ashwin. He was quiet; perhaps he had understood my fears. He would come to the house early in the morning; have breakfast with the entire family, with Nikki sitting next to him at the table, chattering away, asking him questions about Delhi, the places to see. She had heard Reena tell her about Appu Ghar and Red fort in Delhi. She asked Ashwin if she and her Mumma could see that. Ashwin looked at me, but I pretended that I had not heard. Later in the afternoon he took Vishu and Nikki with him and Ma was with me, asking about my life in Dalhousie and my source of income. I told her about my books. She seemed to have read all my books and appreciated my handling of the plot and situations. While we talked about various things, Ma brought the topic of Nikki's schooling. She was already enrolled in pre-school section of a well-known convent school in Dalhousie. Ma was happy that she was in a good school.

Many times during those days I detected that Ma wanted to talk about my future also. She must have felt sorry for me because quite often she would apologize for the pain she and her family; which I presumed meant her son had caused me. I warmed up to the grand old lady who had so much class and sensitivity.

One day Ashwin came over for dinner, not wishing to meet him, I had excused myself from dinner on the pretext of having an upset stomach. I was in my room typing away a chapter of my book on the laptop. Ma entered my room quietly with a bowl of 'khichidi' and had brought some homemade curd. I was moved by her concern and thanked her. She sat with me on the couch and forced me to eat. Later on, she took my hand in hers and said something which filled my eyes with tears. "In the matters of heart, women receive all the bruises while men remain unscarred." Yes I had received maximum wounds, loneliness and humiliation. But was I to be blamed for all this? Suhasini had told me on the day I had informed her of my pregnancy, "Sukriti, you will receive all the brickbats in this affair while your man will go scot free."

Ashwin had moved on from one ministry to another, rising higher and higher in his career, unblemished, with the image of a family man. Many people would have been envious of him, family name, good looks, a bureaucratic wife, and a rich mother, he had everything. What had I got!

Despite my education, my once flourishing career and fame, I had thrown it all away. Though I had promised myself that I will not blame anyone for my loneliness because it was my choice, there were weak moments when I felt emotionally vulnerable and wanted to blame Ashwin for my condition.

Ma had seen the tears in my eyes. She said nothing and left the room. Before leaving for his house Ashwin told Nikki that he wished to speak with me if I had no objection he could come to my room. Nikki came running into my room, "Mamma, Baba wants to speak with you. Can he come?" I said yes he may come. Ashwin entered my room and remained standing. I went on pressing the keys not knowing what sentence I was typing. He said, "I believe you are leaving tomorrow?" I nodded.

"Will you allow me to meet Nikki?" I nodded again.

"Should I come to Dalhousie to meet her?" I looked up sharply, "No, you will not visit us there. I don't want tongues to wag, people know you."

"Will you bring her to Delhi once in a while?" I kept quiet.

Then again he said, "I beg you to let me meet my daughter sometimes. I will come wherever you ask me to come to meet her." I was silent

This so infuriated him that he walked menacingly towards me, I stood up and he held both my shoulders in a tight grip and shook me. "Damn it what do you want? You have taken all the decisions in our relationship and like a love sick boy I followed your tenets. It was your decision to sever our relationship. You disappeared with my child in your womb. How helpless I must have felt when I could not find a trace of you or my child. How much more will you punish me? I have suffered as much as you have suffered, Sukriti. Now let us call truce and for the sake of our daughter find a way where she could have the love of her mother and father both. You owe it to your child." He was exhausted and breathing hard.

I was aware of his heart condition; had not he already had two massive attacks! I told myself that I should not agitate him further. "Okay, let me go back to Dalhousie. I will call you and tell you how you can meet Nikki, but please be careful. I don't want public exposure of this relationship. Besides this you have to consider your public image and marriage."

He winced at the sting in my last sentence. I had not meant it to be a barb but perhaps my bitterness had forced it out. "My marriage has ceased to be of any importance to me or to Radhika. We are two strangers living under the same roof and if you had not disappeared like a chicken everything would have been rectified by now. I would have resigned and asked Radhika for a divorce even given her all my property I owned. You ran away," Ashwin said accusingly. He was speaking the truth.

Next day I left Delhi, Reena, Sadanand and Ma accompanied us till the airport. When we went for the security check, Ma hugged me and Nikki. My daughter had become so fond of her that she was inviting her to come with us. Reena and Sadanand were also sad.

CHAPTER 11

My life in Dalhousie could not return to normal. There was restlessness within me. I could not concentrate on any work; I tried to resume my writing, except writing my thoughts in my diary I could not write anything. After leaving Nikki at the play school, I took to wandering on Mall Road, just looking at people and at shops but not able to focus my mind. What was happening to me! Was it the symptoms of depression! Did I need counseling! My body felt as if it had no strength. I would occasionally feel a numbing feeling in my lower back. I was having strange dreams would wake up all in sweat and tingling sensation in my spine.

One morning Sabi's call came informing me that father had suffered a brain stroke and was in coma. This was the saddest news I could have endured at this point. One part of me wanted to be with my father but I did not want to take Nikki with me, I did not wish to expose her to the curious looks of my relatives. I called up Reena and told her my predicament. She promised to find a solution. Sure enough after two hours Ashwin called me, expressing his sympathy and suggesting that since he was planning a private trip to Goa where he had some close friends, he could take Nikki with him and this will give them an opportunity to spend some time together. I asked Nikki if I could go and meet some friends and she could go with 'Baba' to see the sea and sand and play around. She did not want to go without me. "Mumma you also come you, Baba and I will have great fun." I had to explain to her that a friend was seriously ill and I had to see him. She saw my sad expression and gave her consent.

I called Ashwin and he said that he will come to Dalhousie and drive me till Pathankot from where I can take a flight to Delhi and he would directly fly to Goa with Nikki. He told me that Ma would be joining them in Goa. I was happy for Ma, she will have some time with Nikki and Nikki will grow closer to her father and grandmother. Ashwin took the afternoon flight from Delhi to Pathankot and hired a taxi from there; by late in the night he was in Dalhousie. I had already directed him to my house. He saw my house and liked it immensely, without realizing what he was saying, he said, "This was the kind of location I had visualized where you and I could live peacefully with our child." He sighed sadly and entered the living room. Nikki had just gone to bed. I woke her up and to my pleasant surprise, as she saw Ashwin, she ran to him and he lifted her in his arms, kissing her. I left them alone and went to lay the table. Ashwin was very impressed with the house and suggested that I should ask the owner to sell it to me. I was also thinking since many weeks to broach this subject to Reena. Over dinner Ashwin asked me detailed report of Nikki's health, medicines. I gave him the pouch carrying all her emergency medicines. I had already packed her bag, Ashwin told me just to give her toiletries and one or two dresses because Ma had already bought nice beach dresses for her, which were lying in his bag.

We had to leave very early in the morning. I had my flight for Delhi at 8:30 a.m. and his flight was at 10 o'clock. He would drop me at the airport and then spend two hours with an old acquaintance in Pathankot who was a leading timber merchant. He opted to sleep on the couch in the living room but Nikki insisted that she would sleep with him so he had to occupy my bed, while I went to sleep on the couch.

I was in constant touch with Sabi, she told me that my father's condition was critical and I should come soon. "Don't worry about Ajay and Ganesh, you will be coming for your father," Sabi said. At about 2:00 a.m. my cell phone rang, I guessed what it would be. It was Suhasini telling me that, "Father is no more, and he died five minutes back. Cremation will take place at about 3:00 p.m. today. You will reach by then?" Suhasini was trying to control her sobs. I began to weep. She hung up. I wept uncontrollably. I had lost my dear father, whose sensibilities I must hurt immensely by becoming a mother out of wedlock. In the last four years I had spoken to him only once, the day Nikki was born. He used to send me his blessings through Sabi and Suhasini. "Please Papa forgive me, for all the pain I have caused you." I prayed fervently as I sat in the darkness, crying and remembering my father, and also my mother.

I was truly an orphan now. I may not have lived with my father since a long time but I loved him and respected him for his dignified ways. I heard Ashwin get up, he was going to the bathroom, he must have heard sniffing sounds, he came into the room and in the light thrown by the streetlight he saw me sitting huddled up upon the carpet. He immediately came to me. I gave him the news. He sat down beside me and put his arms around me. He kept stroking my head as I wept. He helped me to rise to my feet and led me to another bedroom and put me in bed. I lay down holding his hand. He kept consoling me, exhausted with weeping I fell into fitful sleep. It was the ringing of the alarm that woke me up. I tried to get up but I could not, my head was resting on Ashwin's arm as he lay stretched by my side on the bed. I gently disengaged myself and went to freshen up. I quickly prepared two mugs of tea and some milk for Nikki and woke Ashwin up. He looked at my swollen red eyes but said nothing. I woke up Nikki and gave her milk. We had to leave in one hour's time. I got Nikki ready. Ashwin had his bath. Neema and her husband prepared breakfast for us and packed it in a hamper.

Before leaving the house I went into my bedroom looking for my reading glasses. Ashwin followed me. I looked at him in surprise. He handed me a thick yellow colored envelope filled with currency notes and before I could return it to him, he took me in his arms and held me against his chest. "Sukriti, I have never stopped loving you. Remember you are the mother of my child, I will love you till my last breath. Keep the money you will need it there." He kissed me on my forehead and released me, and then he went out of the room. In my state of mind a little sympathy was enough to start a fresh bout of weeping.

On the way we remained silent. Nikki was the only one talking and pestering her father with questions. He had great patience with her. We were occupying the back seat. I slept throughout the journey to Pathankot, my head resting on Ashwin's shoulder. At Pathankot I bid a tearful farewell to Nikki. Ashwin hugged me as I took his leave, telling me that I need not worry about anything.

My brother's house was filled with mourners as I alighted from the Taxi, religious rites were being performed. Anshul was the first one to see me. He came towards me and put his arms around my shoulder. I was crying bitterly. Sabi and then Suhasini met me. We hugged each other and cried. Ajay was sitting with the Pundit going through some rites. He looked at me and nodded sadly in my direction. Ganesh was aloof; he pretended not to have seen me. Their wives came to meet me. Courteous but inquisitive, Srinivas asked me softly where I had kept Nikki. I made an excuse that she was with my friends. My father's cremation took place at the appointed time and all male members of my family, my cousins and close male relatives returned late in the evening from the cremation ground. By this time except my close relatives, all had gone away. I was sitting in a corner with Suhasini, teary eyed. My father's enlarged photograph had been placed on a low stool and an oil lamp was burning before it. I kept looking at his picture. How peaceful, how dignified my father was. I silently asked for his forgiveness again. My father's sister Durga aunty came to sit with me. She was my father's youngest sister and my parents had performed all the religious rites at her wedding. As a child I was very fond of her. Durga Aunty talked of good old days, my sisters remembered their childhood with Papa and Mummy. The whole atmosphere was very poignant. Ganesh had not entered the room, perhaps he was avoiding me. Suhasini and Sabi sat beside me very protectively daring anybody to ask me any personal question. Even my sisters-in-law were very guarded in talking to me. Later that night Ajay handed me a sealed envelope. It was addressed to me, I recognized Papa's writing. I opened it in front of Suhasini, Srinivas, Sabi and Anshul. It was a letter, the letter was brief and to the point.

'Dear Sukriti,

My days are drawing near. I had hoped that before death, I would see your child and be able to meet you. But I am afraid to call you and your child home. I shall not subject you to more humiliation than you have already suffered. As a token of my love for you and your child I have prepared a gift deed in your daughter's name, of my house situated in Pachim Vihar Phase II. You will find the details in the document enclosed with this letter. This house is worth a few crores. Sell it; the money will come handy in educating your daughter.

God bless you,

Your loving
Papa.

My eyes became blurred with tears. Both my sisters were happy that Papa had thought of my child. There was no bitterness in them that he had not bequeathed them anything. Ajay called me in his room the next morning to tell me about my mother's ornaments, that she had kept aside for my marriage. He had made a list of all gold and silver items and wanted me to take them out from the locker which he held jointly with my father. He did not ask me about Nikki, I did not tell him anything. Only my sisters were concerned. They were advising me to find a nice man to settle down with and who will also accept Nikki. "Life can get very lonely, Suku," Sabi said. I had a strong urge to tell them the identity of Nikki's father but I was too afraid of this getting leaked out.

Delhi weather is very pleasant in the month of November. I was sitting in the balcony on the first floor when Srinivas came. He said he was looking for the book he was reading, but I know he was looking for an opportunity to speak with me alone. He asked me a straight forward question, "Who is Nikki's father?" I was taken aback, "I don't wish to disclose his identity," I said.

"I am asking you to confirm my knowledge of the identity of this man," Srinivas said.

"What do you know?" I asked nervously.

"Sukriti I will tell you the truth without beating around the bush. After you told Suhasini about your pregnancy I had a mind to meet you personally and urge you to marry this man. I was in Mumbai in connection with a seminar. I wanted to surprise you so I came to your apartment unannounced after the meeting, thinking that I will take you out for dinner and we will talk. I saw a well-dressed tall man climbing up the steps. I was wondering why he had not taken the elevator. When I was getting out of the elevator I saw this man at your door and you came out and hugged him. I had not seen his face. I had a strong intuition that he was the father of your unborn child. I came down again and sat in the lounge on the ground floor. After one hour I saw the same man come down the steps, this time he passed by me and I recognized him. Mr. Ashwin Solanki, the minister. After that I went away deeply disturbed because I knew he was a married man and politically well connected. Few weeks after this, I met him at a function organized by the Medical Association of Delhi. He was the chief guest; his brother-in-law Dr. Sadanand was also present at the function. Sadanand was my course mate in Bangalore Medical College and we were good friends. We renewed our contacts and after that we have been meeting frequently whenever

I happen to come to Delhi. I met Mr. Solanki a number of times at Sadanand's house. He struck me as a good human being. I found out a lot about him, his family and his marriage. I like him."

His revelation took my breath away. He had known all along yet he had not spoken a word about it. I thanked him for respecting my privacy and told him everything right from our meeting to the visit of Mr. Bhaskar, my decision and the recent meeting. I also told him that Nikki was with him in Goa. First time in many years I felt a load lifted from my heart, at least someone in my family knew my secret. We talked for a long time. He knew about Ashwin's heart condition from Sadanand. "Sukriti I am glad you have allowed him to meet Nikki. After all he never cheated you. He had wanted to give up everything for you." Sabi came up at that moment, after that I did not get any time to be alone with Sriniwas before my departure.

Ma called me on the second day to pay her condolences. She assured me that Nikki was happy and spending all her waking hours with her father, they were inseparable from each other. This made me happy but also worried me.

After observing the fourth day of my father's death we all left. I returned to Dalhousie. Ashwin was to bring Nikki two days later so I had lots of time on my hands. I devoted all my time to complete my book.

CHAPTER 12

Nikki was now seven years old and studying in the third standard. She was meeting Ashwin after every three to four months. Sometimes Reena would come to take her, sometimes Ma would come to take her. Ashwin had not come after that day because I had told him that my servants would recognize him and tongues would start wagging about it, but the truth was, his closeness stirred my feelings for him. I did not want to re-start the chapter I had so painfully closed. He understood my feelings and did not directly contact me. We had fixed his meeting with Nikki; one month in summer vacations she would stay at Reena's house in Delhi and Ashwin would come there regularly to meet her. During festival vacation Reena, Vishu and Ma would go to their ancestral place in Rajasthan and take Nikki with them. Ashwin would join them for one week, of course without Radhika.

Nikki had begun to look upon Ashwin as a father, the place of her father in her life was being filled by Ashwin and there were moments when she would ask me in all innocence, "Where is my Daddy? Cannot I have a Daddy like Vishu has?" At such times I would divert her attention with some joke or funny story. I never told her lies, when she asked me whether her father was dead. I said 'no' he was alive and would come one day. Nikki had told her teachers and all her friends that her father was far-far away and will come one day. Those teachers who had come to know about my identity were too discreet to speak about me. Some old nuns in the convent who had been my teachers also when I was here, they were very fond of Nikki and protected her from any kind of teasing.

Life was passing on at its own pace. I had accepted my loneliness. As Nikki was getting closer to Ashwin and Ma, my loneliness was intensifying because during her holidays she would be with them while I would be left on my own. Ashwin had many times given me hints that I should visit Reena and Ma often. Once he even pleaded that he would take me and Nikki abroad for few months, but I refused so fiercely that he did not press me further. Although there were moments when I wanted him to be with me to love me, the way he used to.

I was writing fiction and my books were selling well. It was around this time that Ma expired. Her death was sudden; she had been in good health. On Reena and Ashwin's insistence, she had celebrated her seventy fifth birthday. Nikki could not go because she was having her annual examination of class IV. She missed Nikki and she even called her later that night and described to Nikki the cake that she had cut and the menu for the party. It was exactly a week after her birthday; she had died in her sleep. The doctors said that it was a massive heart attack. When her old maid had gone to give her morning tea, she had found her lying still. Her death was a sad blow to all her family and I also felt the terrible grief of losing her. Nikki wept uncontrollably when I told her about her death. She was grown up enough to understand the meaning of death. I called up Reena and asked her if I could come and pay my respect to her. I could not speak to Ashwin during the day because he had a line of visitors, Radhika was also there.

Ashwin called me in the evening around 5 o'clock, he was grief stricken. He told me that I should come to Delhi with Nikki for Ma's cremation. "But Ashwin there will be people . . .media . . .questions, my presence, Nikki's presence . . . how is Radhika will get suspicious." I asked, "Why do you have to always be afraid of the world? Nikki is Ma's grandchild, she ought to be here. I have already booked tickets from Pathankot to Delhi. I have already e-mailed you the tickets, take the print out. You just have to take a taxi to Pathankot. Your flight is at 8:00 a.m. Sadanand will come to receive you at Delhi airport." Before I could protest he disconnected.

I was confused, one part of me wanted to go to Delhi to see Ma for the last time and another part was telling me that Nikki's and my presence at such a time may fuel the fire. I began to pack a few clothes for myself and Nikki half-heartedly. The cell phone rang, it was Sadanand, and he had called to tell me that he would be waiting for me at the airport at 10:00 a.m. I told him my fears," Do you really think I should come? It will put you all in an awkward position."

"No, you mustn't think like this. Trust me nothing will happen. I am there to handle the situation. Ashwin is distraught with grief. Yours and Nikki's presence will give him some consolation," Sadanand said.

Our flight landed at Palam at 10:30 a.m. and Sadanand and Vishu were waiting for us. Nikki was happy to see both of them. We drove straight to Ma's house at Ashram Road. There were innumerable cars lined up all along the way. As our car stopped at the gate, my heart started beating, there were politicians, people from media, bureaucrats sitting in the lawn. I saw Mr. Bhaskar sitting with Ashwin, his hand on his shoulder. The moment we entered he saw Nikki first and then me, I could see flicker of recognition in his eyes and he nodded in my direction, Ashwin stood up came towards us and hugged Nikki and then gently put his arm around my shoulders. My eyes turned towards Mr. Baskar he was looking at the scene with curious expression, I could sense that those who recognized me were surprised by my presence. I moved away from Ahwin Sadanand saw my discomfiture, he held Nikki's hand and with one hand under my elbow he ushered us into the house.

Ma's body was being prepared for cremation and as per the Hindu rites women were bathing her body. Reena being the daughter was not allowed to take part in this ritual. As Reena saw me she began to cry and I hugged her, trying to console her. Nikki was too frightened by the scene, she started crying. Radhika entered the room and saw me. I could see her expression of surprise in her eyes, and then she saw Nikki, for a long time she looked at her. Reena took me to another room. She was trying to shield me from the curious eyes of the visitors. When Ma's body was fully decorated with flowers, it was carried out in the lawn. The mourners gathered to pay their last respects. I saw Ashwin wearing a white kurta-pyjama standing in the middle of the lawn acknowledging the condolences of the people. Nikki saw him and asked me if she could go and talk to him. I told her that he was busy and she could meet him afterwards. Some more rites had to be performed and the pundits said that the sons, daughter-in-law and the grand children should put garlands and touch Ma's feet. Ashwin was called; Radhika also came and stood next to him. Vishu being the grandson was also made to perform some ritual. I stood away from this holding Nikki's hand. When suddenly Sadanand came towards me and led me and Nikki towards Ma's body. He made Nikki stand with Vishu and touch Ma's feet. Radhika was watching this very intently. Ashwin came closer to both the children and put his arms around them. I could see some flash bulbs; the media could not miss such an opportunity to click. Reena stood by my side sobbing softly. I could feel her pain.

Ma's body was taken for cremation. All men accompanied the body and women stayed behind. Reena took me to Ma's bedroom and we sat there talking about Ma. Nikki and Vishu were both taken by Sadanand with him to the crematorium. Radhika entered the room and I stood up out of respect. She sat down on the 'diwan' while Reena and I were sitting on Ma's bed. We were silent for a long time. I was lost in my own thoughts though I could occasionally hear Reena's sniffing. Radhika at last broke the silence, "Were you acquainted with my mother-in-law?" "Yes, briefly, I had met her at Reena's house," I answered. "Oh! I see," she said. Her cell phone was constantly ringing and she got busy answering the calls.

Later Reena and I went into the lawn and sat under the shade of the tree. We must have dozed off sitting on the lounge chairs; it was the sound of cars that woke us up. Men had returned from the cremation ground. Ashwin, Sadanand, Ashwin's male relations from Rajasthan and some of his colleagues went into the living room. Reena and I went into the kitchen to get the tea ready for all. I helped the servants to cook some light meal for the visitors and laid the table. Radhika was nowhere to be seen. Ma's maid Tara said that she had seen Radhika leave in her car. She had gone home to change into fresh clothes. I was looking for Nikki and Vishu to serve them lunch. I entered a room thinking that the children would be there. I found Ashwin lying on the bed; I was about to turn back and leave the room when he opened his eyes. He got up from the bed and came towards me. I stopped; I could see the signs of sorrow on his face. I knew how close he was to his mother. "Sukriti, Ma has gone. She kept remembering you and Nikki. She was thankful to you for giving her a grandchild. She loved Nikki very much," Ashwin said.

"Nikki is also sad. Ever since I told her about Ma's death, she has been very sad."

"Yesterday Mr. R.C. Vithal, Ma's lawyer told me that Ma had drawn a will a few months back and it was her wish that the will be read in the presence of her family after she has gone, "Ashwin said. "Oh! I see," was all I could see. This was their family matter. "You and Nikki are also Ma's family, so you both have to be present when the will is read," he said, and before I could protest he held my hand, "Why do you have to defy me.

Please Sukriti let us not argue." He went back to his bed and turned his back towards me. I left the room.

Radhika returned bringing a servant along with her to help in the house. I was feeling very uncomfortable in the house with both Radhika and Ashwin around. Reena realizing my state suggested that we should go to her house for the night. When Ashwin heard this, he was annoyed. "For the sake of Ma, let us stay together for a few days till the mourning period is over, why do you want to go home Reena?" Reena did not answer and we had to stay there. Ma's house was a spacious house with wide open space in front of her house and also at the back.

Next day Vishu and Nikki were in the sitting room playing some video game. I wanted to avoid meeting Radhika and Ashwin, so I chose a quiet and secluded corner of the back lawn to sit. Reena and Sadanand were in Ma's bedroom resting after lunch. I closed my eyes and must have fallen asleep in the chair, when I was woken up by Vishu, "Aunty Nikki is feeling sick, she just vomited and she is crying." I ran towards the sitting room. Nikki was lying on the carpet crying, "I am feeling very sick. My stomach is aching," she said as she saw me. I sat down on the carpet with her. Vishu called his parents and Reena and Sadanand examined her. "It is indigestion," Sadanand said and gave some medicine. He picked up Nikki and took her to Ma's bedroom and put her in bed. He instructed me to watch over her, I sat with Nikki the whole afternoon while she slept peacefully. Ashwin had many visitors during the evening and I don't think he was told about Nikki's illness. Radhika did come into the room when she came to know that Nikki was unwell, she inquired of her health and asked me if I needed anything. I had always admired Radhika for her courteous behavior, she may not have much liked me but she never showed it. Radhika was talking to me when Ashwin came into the room. "Sukriti what is the matter with Nikki? Reena just told me that she is unwell." I was nervous, Oh God! Let him not blabber anything before Radhika. I was sure he had not seen Radhika because she was standing near the window and Ashwin could not see her from there. "Thank you Mr. Solanki, Mrs. Solanki has also come to find out about Nikki," I said. He looked around and saw Radhika. He did not flinch or seem surprised but he went towards Nikki's bed and touched her forehead tenderly, "She has fever," he said and asked me to call Sadanand. His behaviour was frightening me because Radhika was watching him. Sadanand took Nikki's fever, it was mild fever caused by the stomach infection. Just at that time Nikki opened her eyes, seeing Ashwin sitting on the edge of her bed sat up, put her arms around his waist calling him 'Baba' and closed her eyes again. Sadanand looked at me and I avoided looking at anybody and kept my eyes downcast. I did not see Radhika's reaction. Ashwin not caring about anyone took Nikki in his lap and held her against his chest, "Baby you are going to be alright. Take this medicine and tomorrow you will be fit and fine and then I will take you and Vishu to Haridwar. You know we have to immerse Ma's ashes in the holy river of Ganga," he said to Nikki. The thought of Ma's ashes made me very sad and Nikki also sobbed. I left the room. Later Reena told me that Ashwin sat there with Nikki in his lap for a long time, till she fell asleep. He left the room after making sure that Nikki was sleeping soundly. Radhika had left the room soon after me.

During the night Ashwin came to check on Nikki finding me wide awake, he sat in the chair by Nikki's bedside looking lovingly at me. He made a remark that nearly took my breath away, "Nikki sleeps just like you do. In your friend's apartment in Delhi I used to wake up in the night and watch you sleeping, your peaceful expression was so endearing, Sukriti," he sighed. Before leaving the room he came towards my side on the bed and bending down over my face he touched my forehead with his lips. "Don't worry my darling, I shall always be there for you both," he whispered and was gone. He had this habit of disturbing my peace of mind when I was putting my emotions in some semblance of order.

I did not see Radhika the following morning. She did not appear for breakfast also. Her servant informed Reena that, "Madam had gone home at night." Just as the lunch had been laid Radhika arrived, looking beautiful in a pale white saree, with a string of pearls around her neck. Radhika was usually reserved. Ashwin, Sadanand were in the sitting room and Reena and I were in the dining room. I was feeding Nikki soup as she entered. She did not greet me or look at Nikki but asked Reena if she had called Ashwin for lunch. At the dining table she took her seat to the right side of Ashwin and kept serving him, while he ate in silence. I was sitting next to Vishu and he was narrating some programme he had seen on Discovery Channel. Reena and Sadanand were listening to his narration very attentively. Nikki was sitting on the other chair silently watching Ashwin and Radhika. I looked at her and she smiled at me. She was wise for her age and never asked uncomfortable questions. So I felt relaxed whenever she was in the company of Ashwin. She seldom called him Baba or showed any intimacy with him when Radhika was around.

Only the previous day she had let her guard down. I was afraid that she must have made Radhika suspicious.

Ma's lawyer arrived as per the appointment. I did not wish to remain present while the will was being read. I excused myself and took Nikki with me to the kitchen garden and sat there with her, telling her about the different plants growing there and how they acquire their colors. Vishu came looking for us, "Mama is calling you and Nikki," he said. I was getting angry with Ashwin, why must he drag me into his family matters! Reluctantly, I went into the sitting room. Reena and Sadanand were sitting with Ashwin, quietly. Ashwin had some papers in his hands and Radhika looked extremely angry as she saw me enter the room. She looked contemptuously at me. The lawyer had gone. Ashwin at last lifted his eyes from the papers and said, "Sukriti, Ma has left a sizeable portion of her assets for Nikki and some for Vishu." I felt my legs would not support me, so shaken did I feel. Why did Ma do such a thing! Did she not realize how it will disturb Ashwin's life?

"This is very kind of Ma. But I cannot accept it. You are her family, you should get it," I mustered enough courage to say this. Radhika looked at me with a strange expression. Reena came to stand by my side. "Ma always looked upon you as own her daughter and she had great affection for Nikki, so it must have given her happiness to leave something for Nikki," she said boldly and cast a daring look in Radhika's direction. Ashwin read out Ma's will which was brief and to the point, mentioning how she wanted her assets to be divided after her death. Her Ashram house she willed to Nikki who on gaining maturity shall become the sole owner of this house until then Ashwin, Ma's eldest son Ashwin Solanki was to be the custodian of her assets. Ma's jewelry was to be given to Nikki at the time of her marriage. Ma's other assets in the form of fixed deposits, shares in leading companies and National saving certificate all amounting to some five crores was to be divided into two, one half would go to Vishu and the remaining was to go to Nikki. Ashwin was to be the legal guardian of Nikki's financial interests and Sadanand and Reena jointly were to be custodians of Vishu's assets. Vishu was also given some residential plots situated in Delhi. Ma had added a line to her will, "My love and blessings to Sukriti, she will one day understand the logic of my gift to Nikki." Ma had also mentioned Ashwin and Reena in her will. "God has given them everything. They don't need anything from me except love and good wishes." The will stirred me from deep within. Ma had been so fair in her largesse, without explicitly mentioning her relationship with Nikki; she had left no doubt in the minds of people that Nikki was as dear to her as Vishu.

There was an eerie silence in the room. Sadanand was the first to walk out of the room, on, the pretext of going to his hospital, he left the house. Reena took me out of the room. Vishu had taken Nikki with him to his house to get some clothes for himself and his mother. Ashwin and Radhika were still in the sitting room. Ashwin was going over Ma's will again and we heard Radhika say something in a sharp voice. Ashwin did not respond. After sometime we again heard Radhika shouting, "You think I am a fool that I don't see through your mother's trick, leaving so much to a stranger! You want me to believe this!" Ashwin's voice, "Well whether you like it or not Ma had every right to give away her assets the way she wanted." "No!" shouted Radhika, "It is not assets I am interested in but I want to know Ma's relationship with that girl and her mother. Last night you were getting crazy with anxiety over that girl's illness and she clung to you calling you Baba." "What do you want to know about Nikki? She was as dear to Ma as her own grandchild would have been. Since you gave her none she was bound to look for comfort elsewhere," I heard Ashwin say. "Don't you dare accuse me? It was your fault that we could not have children," Radhika retorted.

"Radhika, how long will you play this silly game with yourself? You know there is nothing wrong with me. I am capable of fathering children. You are so insecure that even after twenty two years of marriage you cannot face the truth," Ashwin spat.

"That does not answer my question about that girl and her mother!" Radhika said. "Stop calling Nikki 'that girl'. Show some class if Ma loved her and wanted to do something for her, who are we to sit in judgment over her actions. Now this chapter should end here, I don't want further discussion on this," Ashwin said and stood up.

Radhika came after him. She was crying and shouting, "You have to answer my questions. If you don't, I will ask this woman, why is she here, why is her child so important to your family?" Ashwin said calmly, "What do you want to know about Nikki or her mother?" I don't know what Ashwin was going to say but Reena came charging out very angry. "Please Radhika, Sukriti is my dearest friend and Nikki is like my own child, stop insulting them in my mother's house. You have a problem with them, you can leave this house." Radhika lost her cool, "Don't you dare speak to me like this. Truth always hurts. You may try to shield your friend and call her child as you own but the fact is the child will always be an illegitimate child."

Her words pierced my heart. I had never looked at this issue in this light. Children whether born in the wedlock or out of wedlock will always be innocent. Ashwin was shouting, "Radhika, enough of this nonsense. You could never become a mother yourself; you don't have feelings for another's child. I have always been considerate about your feelings. I spent many years of my life with you, out of respect for those years show some grace. You want to know about Nikki's father, well she has a father who loves her dearly and would do anything for her, but his circumstances prevent him from marrying her mother. Now go home and there is no need for you to come here." He sent for the driver and forced Radhika to go home.

I was feeling extremely depressed. I told Reena that after Ma's ashes were collected and taken to Haridwar, I would also like to leave. When Ashwin heard this he came to the room where I was sitting, my eyes red with weeping. I was regretting meeting Ashwin again, coming here and destroying my peace of mind. "Sukriti, this house belongs to Nikki and as her mother you have every right to live here. As far as Radhika is concerned, forget about her." It was not possible for me to forget the words Radhika had used for Nikki, truth hurts and in this case it had hurt me deeply. Radhika had spoken the truth. Nikki was growing up, sooner or later she would be faced with similar situations. How will she cope? My Nikki was a very sensitive girl; she was easily hurt if someone was rude to her. How would I protect her from malicious gossip?

Radhika did not visit the house till I was there. Next day Ashwin, Sadanand, Vishu and some of their close friends went to Haridwar to immerse Ma's ashes. Ashwin wanted to take Nikki but looking at my silent face he did not press, but before leaving for Haridwar he spent some time with Nikki in his room. Nobody was allowed to enter the room. When he and Nikki came out, she looked very happy and he looked relaxed. In the absence of men in the house, Reena decided to sort out Ma's things and send away her clothes to the home for destitute women. I helped her in making separate packages of woolens and shawls. She asked me if I would like to have something of Ma's belongings. I chose an idol of Lord Krishna which Ma kept by her bedside and a book of holy 'Geeta'. Reena put her expensive sarees and shawls in suitcases, "I will send them to Dada's house. He will deal with them," she said. Later that day I requested Reena to let me return to Dalhousie because I was feeling uneasy; there was this terrible restlessness in me, as if something was going to happen. She understood my state of mind and I called up my travel agent to have two seats booked for me by the evening flight that day to Pathankot.

Nikki was unduly quiet on the flight, I asked her, "Darling why are you so quiet? Is there something wrong?" "No Mumma, I am okay," she said and lapsed into silence. Nikki was becoming an introvert like me. She found it difficult to share her feelings with anyone. "Nikki what did you and Baba talk about before he left for Haridwar?" I asked, I was curious to know what he had discussed with his daughter. "Nothing," Nikki replied.

I was happy to be home in my peaceful surroundings. Nikki was back in school. I resumed my writing but somehow I could not concentrate on what I was writing. Ashwin called up, he was very hurt that I had gone away and not even waited for him to return. "Why you did you not wait for me? I returned feeling absolutely lonely. Ma's last remnants have gone. I thought yours and Nikki's presence in the house would give me some solace," Ashwin sighed as he said those words. "I am sorry, I was feeling depressed. I had to go away from there. I feel wretched that your wife has been subjected to pain, for no fault of hers. If anyone is to be blamed for this sorry state, it is you and I, but why should Radhika and Nikki suffer?" I said. "Sukriti, don't blame yourself. We are mere puppets in the hands of our destiny," he tried to console me. I told him that under the circumstances I cannot accept Ma's bequeath to Nikki. "I don't want to cause any more pain and embarrassment to your wife." He was angry and accused me of disrespecting Ma's wishes. "For god's sake, have some sense, it is between my daughter and me you keep out of it," Ashwin said angrily and hung up.

Two months passed since Ma's death, I remembered her every day and Nikki often spoke about her. The time she had spent with her grandmother over the last three years had made her very fond of her. After dinner Nikki and I would sit in the living room, talking about Nikki's school, her friends, my school days, Reena aunty, my family. One night I was feeling restless more than the usual, I attributed this feeling to the mild fever I was running since two days. I had taken some medicine also. Earlier in the day I had felt some pain in my lower back, my joints and shins. Now the pain was coming intermittently although it was bearable, I felt that I should lie down. Next morning my back was stiff and I could barely manage few steps around the house. Neema and her husband came to help and I told them to escort Nikki to her school. I lay down, Neema urged me to see a doctor. She even brought a contact number of a local doctor. Just to appease her, I promised to make an appointment with the doctor and have my pain seen to. When I woke up I felt my pain had subsided so I forgot about seeing the doctor.

One week later while I was walking in the afternoon towards Nikki's school to pick her up, I felt the pain return, this time it was intense pain. I quickly called Neema and told her to fetch Nikki from the school, while I took a rickshaw to go to the doctor's clinic. The doctor was an elderly gentleman, retired army doctor. He examined me thoroughly and suggested some tests to ascertain the cause of the pain. He gave me some pain killers to help me with the pain. "Ma'am, you must have these tests. I see some blue marks on your body, we must ascertain why they have developed. You will have to go to Pathankot medical college for these tests. Don't delay," was his parting remark.

Pain killers did give me momentary relief, but the pain persisted. I was beginning to get worried not for myself but for Nikki. 'What will happen to her should something ever happen to me?' I kept thinking. I did not want to worry Reena with my health problem; she had taken Vishu to Bangalore for his Medical college entrance test. I called up my brother-in-law Srinivas and told him about the tests the doctors had suggested. He was thoughtful for some time and told me that he was coming to Dalhousie with Suhasini after three days; they will take me to the medical college in Ludhiana to have these tests. I was alarmed, "Is there something serious?" "Don't be silly, these are routine tests needed to diagnose the cause of your pain," Sriniwas said to quell my fears.

That night Sabi also called to ask about my health. She talked for a long time and before disconnecting she said, "Suku, we all love you and don't think you are alone. Suhasini and Sriniwas will be with you and I will also come as soon as the children finish their entrance examinations". Both her sons were preparing for IIT entrance examination that month. Nikki was happy that her aunt and uncle from Kodaicanal were coming soon.

The pain killers made me feel sleepy. Ashwin called up that night, he was in South Africa attending some conference, Nikki answered the phone and told him about my illness and about Suhasini and her husband's intended visit to 'take Mamma for some tests to Ludhiana.' This must have alarmed Ashwin so much that he called Sadanand who in turn called Srinivas to find out the details.

It was early next morning that Sadanand called me and then Reena called from Bangalore. They wanted me to give them the contact number of my doctor in Dalhousie. I don't know what my doctor had told them but Ashwin called me soon after, "Sukriti, Sadanand is leaving for Pathankot this afternoon and he will immediately bring you to Delhi for check-up. I have called the AIIMS for an appointment. Can you undertake the road journey to Pathankot?" He was very anxious. I told him that there was nothing wrong with me and he should stop fussing over me. "Why did you bother Sadanand, my sister and her husband would be here," I said. "No, Sadanand has told them about the change of plans, they will come to Delhi. I am also returning to India tonight. I will be at the airport to pick you up." Ashwin had planned everything and there was no way he would change his mind. He spoke to Nikki, I don't know what he was telling her but she was continuously looking at me while talking to her father. After the phone was disconnected Nikki came running to me and put her arms around me. "Mama you are not well and Baba told me to take good care of you, now lie down and I will press your back," her words brought a lump to my throat. The fear was gripping my heart, if something were to happen to me . . . . I could not think beyond my fears and each waking moment this thought haunted me.

That day I wrote furiously in my diary, it had been few weeks since I had written anything in it.

That evening Sadanand arrived. He immediately called my doctor and had a long discussion while I pretended to busy myself in the kitchen. He examined the medicine I was having. That night my pain became severe despite the two painkillers I had taken. I turned and tossed in my bed, when I could not bear the pain I came into the sitting room and walked to deaden the pain. Sadanand sleeping in the adjoining bedroom was woken up. He came out and seeing the expression of pain on my face, he made me lie down and pressed my back gently. He kept assuring me that it was not serious and that I would be healthy soon. I had a strong premonition, I told him that I was only worried about Nikki; I made him promise me that he and Reena would adopt Nikki if I were to die. He comforted me and we sat for a long time talking.

We reached Delhi the next day in the afternoon and found Ashwin at the airport waiting for us. He hugged Nikki and I saw that Nikki was happy to see him. My illness had made her very scared. Ashwin held her close to himself for a long time soothing her with words and kisses. Sadanand and I also became emotional. Later I was taken straight to

All India Institute for Medical Sciences. There were more examinations, tests, questions and all through this Nikki, Ashwin and Sadanand were with me. Later the doctors told Sadanand that the report of the tests will be available only the next day. In the meantime more medicines were prescribed. Ashwin sent me and Nikki along with the driver to sit in the car while he and Sadanand remained in the doctor's chambers. I sat in the car and closed my eyes. Nikki sat next to me holding my hand. Later when Ashwin and Sadanand came I saw a grim expression on their faces. Ashwin sat next to Nikki and Sadanand occupied the seat next to the driver. Ashwin stretched his arm over the back of the seat and gently touched my shoulder, I closed my eyes again. I did not want to see the sadness in his eyes. He gently pressed my shoulders and neck with one hand while stroking Nikki's head with another. We were all silent.

We went to Sadanand's house; Reena was to arrive late that night after leaving Vishu with Sadanand's brother for his examination. Sadanand led me straight into the bedroom and made me have medicine as my pain was persisting. I lay down in bed, Ashwin brought Nikki also in the room and he sat on the chair near my bed. The servant brought tea and Sadanand trying to lighten the atmosphere cracked some jokes and we all laughed. There was a strange sadness lurking in my mind. Ashwin was talking with Nikki about his trip to South Africa and the beautiful things he had brought for her. Sadanand had to go to his nursing home and then he had to go to the airport again to receive Reena. Ashwin assured him that he will stay there till their return.

The medicine made me drowsy and I drifted into sleep. It was the pain in my left side of the lower back that woke me up. I opened my eyes, the night bulb was on, Nikki was sleeping on the next bed and as I moved I felt a hard male body stretched behind me. It was Ashwin lying wide awake and pressing my back gently. He felt me stir and sat up so that I could change my side. I guessed that it must be past midnight. Why hasn't he gone home? I tried to open my lips; he put his fingers on my lips and pulled me in his arms. My illness had perhaps made me so vulnerable that instead of pushing him away I clung to him telling him again and again that I was afraid for our daughter. What will she do without me, where will she go? He kept murmuring words of assurance and promised to love me and look after me and our child as long as he was alive. "Sukriti don't be sad please. I will take care of you. Nothing will ever happen to you," he murmured. Finally I told him to go home, "You must rest Ashwin. You have been with us the whole day. Now go home and sleep." "I am not going home. I will stay here", he said with finality and I kept quiet. The whole night I was hovering between pain and sleep. Every time I woke up I found Ashwin awake by my side. I was overcome with love for him.

Next day Ashwin and Sadanand went to AIIMS to collect my report, Reena sat with me. I could see that my illness had shaken her up. She was trying to be brave, she was eagerly waiting for a call from Sadanand but nothing came. Nikki was in the sitting room reading a book. Ashwin and Sadanand returned around lunch time. One look at Ashwin's taut expression confirmed my fears; there was something seriously wrong with my reports. Reena did not ask anything and nothing concerning the reports was mentioned. Nikki was the only person who was talking at lunch. She asked Ashwin about the earthquake which had recently occurred in Chile. He answered her questions patiently. Seeing these two I felt a sense of assurance that Nikki had accepted Ashwin and he had taken the place of a father figure in her life. She looked up to him. At such moments I was always troubled by the fear as to how long will I be able to hide from Nikki her true relationship with Ashwin and how will she react to this truth. Should I tell Nikki when she was a little older about Ashwin?

Ashwin was saying something to me but being lost in my thoughts, I did not hear. Nikki gently nudged me, "Mama where are you?" I found Reena and Ashwin watching me with a strange look on their faces.

It was in the evening while I was resting that Ashwin came to my room. He sat on my bed and took my hand in his hand; he was shaking with suppressed emotions. I watched him intently not sure what he was going to say. "Your medical reports are not very encouraging. You will have to undergo some more tests. Sadanand spoke to your brother-in-law Dr. Srinivas who suggested that you come to Mumbai; there is a best institute where you will undergo treatment. You will be fine; it is just a short treatment. Sukriti, Reena and I will go with you. Your sister and Dr. Srinivas will now come to Mumbai."

Surprisingly I was calm and heard Ashwin very calmly and even nodded my head in consent. Worst had happened in my life. Ashwin sat with me for a long time just holding my hand. We both had one feeling in our hearts, fear of future, fear for our daughter, her upbringing. At last I spoke, "Ashwin, now we have to discuss Nikki's future. I may not be with her for long. Have you thought where will she go, who will take care of her? She has to be told the truth about her relationship with you. I don't want her to grow up with the feeling that she is an orphan."

My words must have caused Ashwin great pain because his eyes became moist. "Sukriti you are going to be fine. I will talk to Nikki and gently reveal the truth to her. She is my daughter and my responsibility, you don't worry. Just take care of your health."

I was not convinced by this. "You have to tell Radhika about your relationship with Nikki. It would shock her but she will accept it when I am gone. She is a good lady; I know she will love her as her own daughter." Perhaps the thought of death had made me bold, otherwise I could have never imagined suggesting such a reckless thing to Ashwin, knowing his entire political career will be destroyed by such a step. He heard me calmly and said, "Radhika is abroad. She opted for a transfer to U.K. She left one week after Ma's death. We haven't spoken to each other after that fight at Ma's house. She is too proud to accept such a situation. I don't want her anywhere near Nikki. I will look after Nikki myself, if anything happens to you. Reena will always be there to help me."

Our conversation was intervened by the ringing of my cell phone. It was Suhasini calling from Kodaicanal. She asked me about my health and lovingly assured me that I had nothing to worry, "These things happen and there is good and effective cure for your illness." She was coming to Mumbai with Srinivas and would stay with her daughter Nevadita in Navi Mumbai. She asked me to come there straight away from the airport. "Suku, Nevadita's house is quite close to the Cancer Research Centre. We will have no problem in commuting, bring Nikki along with you, she will have some company with Nevadita's son." Before disconnecting Suhasini said in an emotionally charged voice, "Suku, we love you and want you to get well." My sister was like that, always forgiving, loving and never judging people from her own point of view and her gem of a husband Srinivas was just like her, trusting and caring. A smile came to my lips and I disconnected the cell phone. Ashwin was happy to see me smile. He had some work at office and he promised to return soon, "We will have dinner together," he said and left. He met Nikki in the sitting room and sent her to be with me.

Next day we left for Mumbai by early morning flight. Reena and Nikki were also with me. Ashwin was to come later in the evening; this was my suggestion because I did not want any public display of our togetherness. Suhasini, Nevadita and Srinivas were waiting for us at the airport. Suhasini could not control her tears the moment she saw Nikki.

She was meeting her for the first time. We hugged and cried. Every time I meet Suhasini I feel my mother has come alive in front of me, the same eyes, complexion and so loving. Nevadita had to put her arms around me and her mother to stop us from crying. Reena and Srinivas were watching us indulgently. Nikki loved this aunt of hers who simply adored her.

The journey although only a few hours from Delhi, had exhausted me. I needed to lie down. Nevadita and Suhasini sat by my bed side as I lay down. Reena and Srinivas were sitting in the study room. I know why they were there; Reena was showing Srinivas my test reports. Later when they both joined us there was laughter and jokes but I could not help detect the traces of sadness in Srinivas's eyes. Suhasini was trying to be cheerful, playing with Nikki and Nevadita's three year old son Lakshya. She kept herself occupied but I knew my dear sister was concerned about my health because she kept coming to my room to check on me. Ashwin called to say that he was coming to Mumbai with an industrialist friend in his friend's private plane since one of his industrialist friends was also coming to Mumbai in his personal plane. Srinivas invited him to stay at Nevadita's house instead of at the state guest house which he accepted. I was not sure how Suhasini would react to my relationship with Ashwin. I told Srinivas about this when I met him alone. He comforted me that there was nothing to fear. He had told Suhasini everything before coming to Mumbai, although she was shocked, she is too good natured to hold grudge for long.

When Ashwin came in, Nikki went running to him and he picked her up in his arms. Suhasini and Srinivas welcomed him warmly and the little apprehension I had felt was also gone. Looking at this scene I felt a sense of contentment that I was surrounded by the people whom I loved dearly and who loved me. I knew my Nikki will be cherished by these people when I am gone. The thought of death was beginning to take a firm grip on my psyche. The word cancer that I had only seen other people suffering from was now gnawing at my body. I had seen my mother die of this dreadful disease now it was my turn. Was it a curse on me for stealing the right of another woman! I would often think about this, these days and remember the famous lines from Macbeth" but in these cases we still have judgment here"

Ashwin, Srinivas and Suhasini talked for a long time in Nevadita's sitting room. Suhasini was sobbing softly, Ashwin was comforting her, "Please don't; you are a doctor, and you should not give up. There is a cure for this. Today I spoke to one of the famous oncologists in USA over the phone; he told me that the disease can be arrested at this stage with chemotherapy." I heard Srinivas, "Yes, we should be positive. Let's see what the doctors say at the Cancer Research Centre."

"Mr. Solanki, what have you thought about Nikki's future, should anything happen to Sukriti?" it was Suhasini bluntly asking him. "If I may call you Suhasini, Nikki and Sukriti are a part of my life. I love Sukriti and Nikki is my only child. I will look after her, but nothing will happen to Sukriti, why are we being pessimistic," Ashwin said and then the topic was dropped.

Later that night Suhasini made Ashwin's sleeping arrangement in my room and I think it was Nevadita and her husband who had suggested it to her. Nikki and Reena were to sleep in the guest room. I had no appetite, the medicine I was having was killing my hunger. Ashwin and Srinivas forced me to have some soup and a toast. Their care was making me so emotional that while sitting at the table, tears began to roll down my cheeks. I had read somewhere that only the dying man knows how precious life is. Reena sitting next to me held my hand; Ashwin stood up from his chair and came near me. I could not control my weeping; I held his hand and cried inconsolably. Suhasini put her arms around me wiping my tears, speaking endearments to me like my mother used to when I had hurt myself. I must have cried for a long time, because in the end I felt terribly drained of all my energy and put my head on the back of the chair and closed my eyes. Thank God Nikki was in the other room playing with Lakshya. Ashwin kept patting my hand. Later he and Srinivas took me to my bedroom and put me in bed. They kept comforting me that I would be healthy again; I had to exert my inner strength to get well. I fell asleep soon after. It was only when Ashwin quietly slipped into bed at some point of time that I woke up. He took me in his arms and held me close. I lay awake feeling his warmth, he was awake thinking.

I said at last, "I have brought only unhappiness in your life, but you have given me so much love that I am eternally thankful to you." "Hush," he said, "You have given up everything for me, your career, your freedom, and your family and do you think I don't realize what price you have had to pay for loving me?" He kissed me gently, careful as not to hurt me. If I had died that moment it would have been the most appropriate death.

Next day Srinivas, Suhasini, Ashwin and Reena took me to the National Cancer Research Centre; two topmost specialists checked my reports. I was subjected to more tests; biopsy was conducted, by first giving me an injection to numb a certain portion of my spine and then a needle inserted to take my bone marrow for biopsy, it was painful and exhausting at the end of it I was not in a position to sit or walk so the doctors took me to a special ward and made me lie down. Reena and Suhasini joined me in the ward. Ashwin, and Srinivas were with the doctors. Suhasini kept holding my hand and Reena was pressing my back. Later I was allowed to go home, Sriniwas drove in silence and Ashwin was sitting by his side. I was at the back with Reena and Suhasini, a little jerk was also causing me terrible pain so we drove slowly. At home Nevadita helped me to walk into the bedroom and I immediately went to sleep. Suhasini brought some lunch and fed me with her own hands.

Nikki was watching the change in me. She would sit near me and keep looking at my face. This made me very sad, "My darling how can I tell you that you may never see me, soon," how soon, I had no idea but I had an intuition that it would not be long. Ashwin was spending all his time with me and Nikki. At night he would put Nikki to sleep and then stay by my side the whole night. Sometimes Suhasini would also keep awake talking to him late in the night. Most of the time it was about Nikki and me. Ashwin would listen to her worries patiently and try to assure her that I would be okay.

My biopsy report came on the third day and it was confirmed that I had bone marrow cancer and unfortunately the stage had gone when it could have been stalled from spreading further. This news brought the whole house to a standstill. Suhasini's eyes were red every time I saw her, Reena was equally sad. The worst affected was Ashwin, I could see in his face an emptiness as if his spirit was broken. That night while putting Nikki to bed his eyes filled with tears, he sat for a long time with her and told her gently that he would always be with her no matter what happened. In my room he was trying to be brave and joked about getting into the habit of sleeping with me, "Madam, you are getting me addicted to you," he said and sighed. I smiled. I knew I had to be bold and courageous and do things I had always wanted to do.

Next day I announced at the breakfast time that I was going back to Dalhousie and complete the book I was writing, "My publisher must be pulling his hair, I am already late," I said. Srinvas insisted that I should stay. "No," I said, "No, I will take pain killers, but I will not live like an invalid. You know my disease is incurable now." Despite his persuasion, Suhasini's tears, Reena's request and Ashwin's coaxing, I stood my ground. "I have to go back to Dalhousie, Nikki is missing her school." I put a brave front and they had to relent. Before our departure from Mumbai Suhasini and Srinivas called everybody for serious talk with regard to Nikki's future. "We intend to legally adopt her if Sukriti consents, her future will be secured" Srinivas said. I looked at Ashwin for his reaction, he said sharply "Nikki is my child and I intend to keep her with me"

Suhasini asked him rather sarcastically "Do you have the guts to publically own her as your child? When all these years you have been leading a dual life."

"Sukriti would not allow me to take any step; she always stopped me from taking any step. It was she who went away and concealed herself and Nikki from any discovery. You ask your sister why she does not want me to acknowledge Nikki as my child." This made my sister more emotional and she began to sob. I had to intervene and tell them that I had already made up my mind about who would take care of Nikki and though I respect their sentiments, they should not worry about her, she will be looked after well.

At that point of time an idea was taking firm root in my mind with regard to Nikki but I was not too certain that it would materialize Therefore when Ashwin later asked me about it I was evasive, not wanting to upset me he did not press me. I could see that he was under a tremendous pressure. Even before leaving for Dalhousie he pleaded with me to come to Delhi where Reena and he could take care of me, "What will you do all alone when the pain gets worse, who will look after you?" Ashwin asked deeply exasperated at my stubbornness. "Neema and her husband are good people they will take care of everything" I said.

I needed to get away and think clearly, in the end Ashwin gave in but threatened to have me forcefully taken to Delhi once my work in Dalhousie was over "You have always won against me this time let me win." He pleaded.

"I don't ever want you to lose. When I am gone you will understand the reason why I did not want you to be publically associated with us." I tried to comfort him. Ashwin hugged me with utmost love when we parted at Mumbai Airport. His flight left before mine and I saw him repeatedly turning to look at me as he left to collect his boarding pass. My parting with Suhasini and Srinivas was equally poignant. I told Suhasini jokingly," Don't weep for me; in my next birth I will be born as your daughter, and then you can control my wildness". She cried some more until Srinivas gently admonished her.

CHAPTER 13

I am back in Dalhousie. I have some important work to do; time is running out for me. I have to write a letter to Radhika. Yes I had to do this. If any woman has the right to be Nikki's mother, it is she. I had seen in her eyes at the time of reading of Ma's will the flicker of understanding about Nikki's relationship with her mother-in-law and Ashwin's concern for Nikki. I remember the pain in her eyes when Ashwin had taunted her about not being able to have a child. Radhika is an intelligent woman with the kind of exposure she has had she will not hold it against Nikki. When I am gone she will be the mother to my daughter. Nikki will have both her parents.

I wrote a brief letter to Radhika, asking for her forgiveness that I have come between her and Ashwin, explaining briefly the circumstances which brought Ashwin and me together and Nikki's conception. I wrote, "Radhika, when I came to know that I was with the child, I was happy not for myself so much as for Ashwin, that he will experience the joy of fatherhood. I went away from Ashwin and broke all my contact, but it was you who inadvertently brought us together again in the hospital. Perhaps destiny had wanted us all to meet. God is my witness that although I love Ashwin dearly, I have never wanted to take him away from you. I can understand your sorrow. Do you have it in your heart to forgive a dying woman, who is requesting you to become the mother to her daughter?"

I posted the letter on her U.K. address which I had got from Ashwin's diary in Mumbai. I am not sure how Radhika would respond. I am also afraid that she may use this letter to ruin Ashwin's career or use it as a ground to blackmail him.

Another entry I made in my diary: Since many days I have been anxious. Ashwin calls me many times a day; I detect nothing from his voice, if Radhika had called him, accused him of betrayal, he would have told me. I had not mentioned the letter to him or anyone. I was worried sick about Radhika's reaction.

Sometimes I would hate myself for giving in to my impulse. Reena is making frequent trips to Dalhousie, Sabi came with her husband, stayed with me and even urged me to leave Dalhousie and live with her or Suhasini. "You will be well looked after," she said. I have made peace with my brothers. I had a gift deed made of my father's bequeath in the name of my brothers and sent them the documents. Ganesh and my elder brother have learnt of my illness, they are both concerned and asked me to come to Delhi and live with them. I am happy that I am going without any bitterness with my brothers. The house Ma had left for Nikki; I refused to accept the will on the ground that it should go to the legal heirs of Ma. I sent those documents to Reena. Whatever money I had in banks I put it in a joint account with Nikki and drew a will that all my bank deposits and the royalty from my books would be my daughter's and until she attains the age of maturity Ashwin Solanki and Mrs. Radhika Solanki would be her legal guardians.

Chapter 14

I have just completed another book. This is going to be my last novel. I am constantly in pain now. Ashwin was pleading with me yesterday to leave Dalhousie and come to Delhi. "Sukriti, please, listen to me. At least, this time. You are all alone there, what if something happens when you are all alone?" he had said in a broken voice. I am not going anywhere. I have told Nikki that I am very ill and I may die but she will not be alone, her Baba, Reena aunty and both my sisters and their families will be by her side. I was surprised when Nikki replied, "Yes Mama, Baba had told me long time back that you are ill. You know what, he also told me one day after Ma's death that he was my father and that he will always be with me." I was surprised that Nikki had known all along about her relationship with Ashwin. Well, I am relieved that things are falling in their place.

Yesterday late in the night I called my servants Neema and her husband and told them that I was very ill and would not live long. I had put a substantial amount of money in their bank account and they would have a comfortable old age. Both began to weep and promised to take care of me and Nikki as long as they were alive. I know in a few weeks' time I would not be able to walk or do much physical activity, I will need these loyal helpers. After this they have become more sensitive to my needs and serve me faithfully. I am mentally very alert. I am on pain killers most of the time. I have lost a lot of weight. Nikki stays by my side all the time except when she is at school.

The nuns from the convent are holding regular prayers for me, every alternate day they come to visit me and we joke and laugh a lot. I am no longer afraid of death. I have made friends with shopkeepers of

Dalhousie. They have become my fans having read some of my books; they have great affection for me and are aware of my terminal illness but they appear quite normal. Fresh supply of fruits and vegetables are being sent to my house with get well cards. I did not know that people liked me so much. In all these years I had kept away from these people but now they have become my greatest friends. The local press also brought out an article on me and my achievements. The national newspaper carried that article in their columns and those who had forgotten me, remembered me. I am receiving cards, letters, all praying for my health. My friends in Mumbai are sending their good wishes through the newspaper columns.

Although I am in pain I am writing regularly in my diary. I have thought about leaving this diary for Nikki so that when she is grown up she will know me better.

Today is Saturday and I am in pain since morning. The local doctor has become my friend so he comes on alternate days, checks my blood pressure and takes a cup of tea with me. But today he came and finding me in bed he checked my blood pressure. He looked alarmed and called Neema and her husband to help me into his car because my blood pressure is falling dangerously and I will have to be hospitalized. I told him that there is no use. He insisted that he will be able to look after me better in the hospital. Nikki called up Ashwin and Reena to tell them that I was not well and was being taken to the hospital. She must have cried in fright. Ashwin was deeply disturbed, he spoke to my doctor.

I think I am writing last pages of my diary. I am in the hospital and it is night time, I wonder if I would live through this night! My fever is running high, my pain is becoming unbearable. Neema is staying with Nikki at home and her husband Tika is with me in the hospital. Two nuns from the convent are also staying with me. I am writing furiously in my diary. I want to record my experiences of each moment of dying. I can see the images of my parents, my sisters, my brothers rising before my eyes. How much pain I must have caused to them, especially to my father, "I promise you papa that I will meet you soon and beg for your forgiveness".

I am hallucinating, at one stage I am seeing Nikki as a small baby crawling towards a cliff; Ashwin running to hold her . . . , I must have shouted that the doctor came running . . . .

CHAPTER 15

Years later Baba gave me this diary to read and asked me to complete the last chapter of my mother's diary . . . .

My mother didn't live to complete the last page of her diary. Her condition deteriorated during the night. The doctors attending on her told the sisters from the convent that the end was near and I should be called. Neema aunty received the call at about 3 O' clock in the morning. She quickly got me ready and we walked towards the hospital. I saw my mother gasping for breath and the doctors were putting an oxygen mask on her mouth. Her eyes were wide open. She saw me and I began to weep, "My baby don't cry," she said and took my hand in hers. From her touch I could feel the life ebbing out of her. I could not see my mother; my strong and beautiful mother looking at me helplessly. I held her hand in mine. Dawn was breaking and my mother lay semi conscious; gasping intermittently for breath.

I had heard the noise of a helicopter. In Dalhousie such noise is unheard of, who has come! I wondered. I sat on mother's bed; tears trickling down my cheeks telling her again and again that she would get better and then we will live like the old times. I heard footsteps approaching our room as if some people were running towards us. As I turned my eyes towards the door I saw Baba entering the room and just behind him, walking with sedate expression was, Radhika Aunty. I gently touched my mother's arm "Mumma, Baba has come and Radhika Aunty has also come with him". My mother opened her eyes. She was finding it hard to focus, she stretched her hand and Radhika held it and said softly, "I have come, Sukriti". My mother smiled faintly, "I have been waiting for you Radhika". She whispered and closed her eyes.

Doctors tried to revive her but she was dead. Radhika Aunty put her arms around my shoulder and took me out of the room. The last glimpse I had of my mother was her white face and peaceful expression as if she was at peace with herself and Baba sitting on her bed ,his face covered by his hands.

My mother was cremated in Dalhousie at the foothills of Upper Bakrota. She could not have found a better place than this for her eternal rest. She was the daughter of hills and had finally found her peaceful abode among the sylvan surroundings of the mountains. I grew up in those few hours and realized that now I was at the mercy of others. My life will never be the same again. Baba would often look at me with eyes filled with sorrow; silently consoling me.

Baba performed the last rites of my mother in the presence of my aunts and the uncles whom I was meeting for the first time. Reena Aunty and Sadanand Uncle took care of me while Radhika Aunty helped Neema Aunty to pack our belongings. She told Baba that Mama's things would be taken with them to Delhi and Reena Aunty will sort them out later. The doctor had found my mother's diary on her bed in the hospital which he handed over to Radhika Aunty, she gave it to Baba . . . .